NOT A MARINE, NOT A SCIENTIST, NOTHING HUMAN.

The head looked to be encased in a metal jacket, but as this thing moved, the metal-like skin of its face moved. . . . shifted . . .

But eyes . . . *Does it have eyes?* Those dozens of whitish things—were they eyes? Though it certainly had a mouth. No doubting that. And the legs—massive, ending in giant wedge-shaped claw feet.

It raised its hands. At least it didn't have any weapons. Still, those claws looked nasty.

An alien, Kane thought. *We have aliens here?*

But even as the thing took a towering step close to him, Kane doubted that.

Aliens. Arriving in spaceships? Was that what was happening here?

He raised the shotgun. Whatever the hell it was, Kane was about to blow it off the walkway when he felt something close around his head.

Peripheral vision told him the bad news: another one of those things had appeared on the walkway behind him.

And now it held Kane's unhelmeted head firmly in its massive hand, squeezing tight.

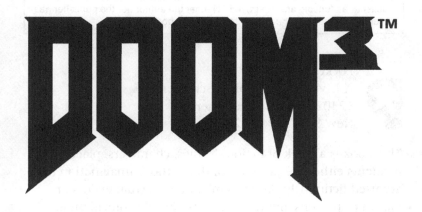

DOOM³™

WORLDS ON FIRE

MATTHEW COSTELLO

BASED ON THE VIDEOGAME
DOOM 3 **FROM ID SOFTWARE**

Pocket Star Books

New York   London   Toronto   Sydney

Pocket Star Books
A Division of Simon & Schuster, Inc.
1230 Avenue of the Americas
New York, NY 10020

First Pocket Star Books paperback edition March 2008

POCKET STAR BOOKS and colophon are registered trademarks of Simon & Schuster, Inc.

For information about special discounts for bulk purchases, please contact Simon & Schuster Special Sales at 1-800-456-6798 or business@simonandschuster.com.

Cover design by Alan Dingman; Art by Robert Hunt

Manufactured in the United States of America

10 9 8 7 6 5 4 3 2 1

ISBN-13: 978-1-4767-9126-5
ISBN-10:   1-4767-9126-0

To Christopher Golden
Good friend and fellow writer—
and my second favorite big guy
from Skull Island . . .

2144

ONE

1

IAN KELLIHER WALKED UP TO WHAT LOOKED TO
be an enormous portal, the steel plates sealed tight.
He tapped it, then turned to the three men following
behind him.

"So—what's on the other side?" he asked.

Two of the men—Elliot Swann, the company lawyer, and Jack Campbell, the head of security—turned
to the man in uniform. Medals and colorful bars
spoke of experience; three stars indicated a general.

A general in the space marines, Kelliher thought. Less
a U.S. government military unit than a Union Aero-
space Corporation private security force.

"Mars," the general replied. "Right now, nothing
but a big flat expanse of red dirt and rock."

Kelliher nodded. He knew the project was behind
schedule, even though no one had told him so. No-

body ever told him the truth about the problems. Nobody ever told him anything they thought he didn't want to hear.

Worst of all, he'd have to go back Earthside and report to his father, the great Tommy Kelliher. Sitting in his castle-like Newport Beach estate, monitored by the best medical help that money could buy, kept alive by drugs and machines that most of the world's hospitals hadn't even heard about.

Tommy Kelliher. UAC founder emeritus.

Ian was now the UAC chairman. But as long as the pumps forced air into his father's lungs, Ian would still have to talk to the man who made UAC the amazingly powerful global business it was today. After all, how many businesses owned an entire planet?

Sure, Mars was being developed as a "joint venture" by the United States government and the UAC, but there was no one on Capitol Hill who didn't know the truth. Mars would be a UAC operation, and the good old U.S. of A. was merely along for the ride.

Kelliher took a step closer to General Hayden.

"General, my supervisors say that the work out there, connecting the units . . . that it's all not going as easily as anticipated."

Hayden nodded. The man had seen his share of battles—or "skirmishes," as the government liked to call the never-ending little wars that plagued planet Earth—so he didn't exactly shrink, or back away a step, but a thin line of sweat broke out on his brow.

"True, there have been difficulties. Some rock formations went much deeper than we thought. The surveys were completely wrong in certain places—"

The other two men stayed quiet. Not their job to add heat to this dish.

"But, General," said Kelliher, "you have done everything you can to help the teams, correct mistakes, to keep us moving forward, yes?"

"Full speed ahead, Ian."

As if we're in the navy now. And not in the middle of the largest construction project ever attempted anywhere, let alone in a hostile environment.

Nothing even came close.

"Good. Full speed, as you say. Okay—so now I want to *see*."

Hayden's eyes narrowed. "See? See what?"

Another tap of the metal. "Outside. The work, the progress, talk to some my supervisors. And—oh yes—" A pause, so Hayden knew what Kelliher's real purpose was. "I want to look around Delta. Best tell Betruger."

Hayden didn't move.

"And how about we get started now, General?"

Hayden nodded, and then turned and started leading the men away from the unfinished corridor and back to the Administration wing.

"This will all eventually be sealed," Hayden said, pointing to a series of airlocks.

Kelliher walked up to them. "They don't look very substantial."

"As I said . . . just temporary, until we have completed the other EVA access points," Hayden replied. "But perfectly safe, of course."

Kelliher fired a look at his lawyer. "Joining us, Swann?"

"That's all right, sir. I can wait—"

"No, really. I insist. Join us," Kelliher said.

Campbell had already gotten into an EVA suit. A frequent visitor to the Red Planet, Campbell had supervised the implementation of the security systems for the ever-growing Mars City perimeter.

Mars City . . .

A prosaic name for such a massive undertaking, Kelliher thought. A city on another planet. And while there would be no towering skyscrapers—in fact, much of the base would be underground—it would ultimately rival many of its counterparts back home in size, scope, and—to be sure—ambition.

Big plans were in the works for Mars City. When it was done, anyway. One of these days.

Kelliher took a suit offered by one of the marines on guard, and immediately felt the weight of it. "We need something this heavy? I thought Martian summer was in full swing."

Hayden pulled on his suit with another marine helping him. "Last night we got hit with icy dust storms from the poles. And in the morning, it's always cold. So we need a heavy suit. Should get warmer by lunch."

Kelliher turned to the climate readout on the side of the EVA ports. Minus 43 degrees. South Pole weather. But here it could get a lot worse, down to minus 250 degrees. And every now and then, at the Martian equator you'd get a balmy 60 degrees Fahrenheit. Short-sleeve weather by Martian standards.

The marine assisting them brought over the lightweight helmets, consisting of a clear headpiece that attached to the compact compressed air tanks fitted into slots in the back.

Not much worse than gearing up for a deep ocean dive, Kelliher thought.

This would be only his second time out on the Martian soil. For some inexplicable reason, he found himself fraught with tension.

The Martian Rover, with its driver in front, sat parked, waiting just outside the airlocks.

"Let's walk instead," Kelliher said.

"Right," Hayden replied, his voice a bit too loud in Kelliher's helmet. "We can walk." Kelliher immediately adjusted the controls on his right forearm. Didn't need the general deafening him.

Even just a few feet away from what would be the Administration Wing, Kelliher could see the immense progress. The Mars City reception area looked nearly done, ready to connect to Admin. And past that—

"That's Security and Combat?" Kelliher asked.

"Yes," Hayden replied. "Marine Command is already based there. The infirmary is up and running. Most of the marines are already bivouacked over there."

"And that?" Kelliher pointed past Marine Headquarters to a large sprawl of construction just to the right and behind it, not yet connected to any of the other bases.

"Alpha Labs. Fully self-sustained. Already operational. Like all the labs."

Kelliher nodded. Each part of the base could exist independently of the others, with air, water processing, even—to some extent—food production. Alpha Labs was already busy carrying out experiments designed to make Mars more sustainable—everything from the implications of low-grav hydroponics to the feasibility of using the great Martian dust storms to increase CO_2 gases and accelerate the greenhouse effect.

The holy grail for Alpha Labs would be to create a breathable atmosphere on Mars. *My God, that would really be something.*

"Looking good, General. I assume the construction team can meet us after the tour?"

"Absolutely. I've invited them all for lunch."

"Fine. Just don't feed them. We're behind schedule enough." Kelliher made that comment flatly; no joke there. Every day they lagged behind schedule kept giant payments from the U.S. government from kicking in. Mars City had to be completed, and soon, or the UAC would start to bleed millions.

Kelliher looked at Hayden. "Just two more things to see now, General. Delta, of course. And the site."

"Yes, sir."

Hayden didn't sound happy. The general never sounded happy when the site was mentioned. *Well, then. Fuck him.*

2

THE BORDER OF THE REPUBLIC OF TEREKSTAN
40.673 DEGREES NORTH LATITUDE,
72.217 DEGREES EAST LONGITUDE

LIEUTENANT JOHN KANE HELD UP HIS RIGHT hand, and the row of armored vehicles trailing behind him came to a sudden stop. So far he had done a fine job of maintaining—as ordered—complete radio silence.

Kane climbed out of his lead vehicle and jumped to the ground. He dug out his standard issue marine "Pete"—a nearly indestructible PDA that did everything but make a cup of joe.

He heard the engines humming behind him, idling, ready to continue their march. But first Kane needed to check exactly where they were. The lieutenant hit a button, then scrolled down to the live map showing their current position.

The screen glowed and then the crazy-quilt image of eastern republics flashed on the screen. He and his squad had just violated one republic's airspace, then trespassed across another's sovereign territory.

Was that republic complicit in what was happening here, or were they too busy with their own dozen skirmishes and revolts to bother with a small U.S. convoy racing across their homeland? Who the hell knew?

He looked at the map while Sergeant Chadbourne came up behind him. "We okay, Lieutenant?"

Kane turned to him. "Appears so. Looks like we just crossed the Terekstan border five minutes ago. Now at least all the other 'stans' can forget about us."

Terekstan was the latest in what appeared to be a domino-like lineup of "stans" that bloomed in this desolate region like some dogged weed—one appeared, then got swallowed by another, while another chunk split off from that.

And fueling the whole mess was the ever-present need for two things: water and oil.

Most of the planet still used fossil fuels—whatever was left, anyway—with the premium alternative fuel sources firmly in the hands of the big corporations. But worse, potable water was no longer commonplace. Two rare commodities had become even more insanely rare, especially now that coastal areas had begun what looked like an inevitable disappearance.

The world had already waved good-bye to most of Florida, so long to the glorious Hamptons. And Africa?

If you thought too long about Africa, the hopelessness of that whole situation could be absolutely overwhelming.

"We're good." Kane looked across the ridge and then down to what seemed to be a rocky plain, stretching to a city—maybe the only city in this new republic. A republic that recently discovered it was sitting on a massive undiscovered oil field. Miles down, but obtainable. And everyone wanted it.

Except this particular mission wasn't about getting the oil—at least not on paper. This one was all about rescue.

"Okay," Kane said. "Let's keep moving . . . eyes on me . . . want to keep radio silence until we're ready to go in."

"Got it, Lieutenant."

Chadbourne walked back to the other vehicles.

In a few minutes, it would be party time. And as was often the case these days, who knew which of them would get out of this thing alive.

Kane could see the city below, tight against the small river that, at one point, was probably its only reason for existence.

Flashes of light popped from within the shadowy outlines of the ancient city. Firefights. Street fighting. Never a fun game to play.

The marines that had been sent in there were there—supposedly—at the request of the Terekstan government. But then things had changed. A better offer had popped up from somewhere, and the government had aligned with the radicals to wipe out the now-invading U.S. troops. *You'd think we would have learned by now,* Kane thought.

Either way—it was time.

Kane slid back into the confines of his AAV—a heavily armored attack and troop vehicle. He looked at the men sitting there, most of whom he barely knew, others survivors of a dozen other skirmishes with Kane. No one looked happy. They were here—like him—because these days a paycheck was a goddamn paycheck.

He popped his earpiece in. The signal and his words would be scrambled on their way to Command, but that wouldn't necessarily prevent anyone from picking the signal up, unscrambling it, and hearing every word.

"Mustang Company in position."

He waited. His words were now being broadcast through one of the dozen situation rooms in the subterranean New Pentagon, its location hidden—though everyone knew it was somewhere in the mountainous West. Away from the constantly rising waters. Away from the crazed cities. Well behind the protective wall of the SW3 defense system.

He waited.

"Mustang, Command Dover acknowledges. Abort mission."

Kane stopped. *Abort mission? They fucking kidding?*

As if to punctuate the moment, Kane heard a series of massive explosions, some real serious and heavy stuff joining the distant popgun sound of fire-fights.

"Request clarification," Kane said.

"Abort mission. Return to the pickup point immediately. Acknowledge order, Mustang."

Just then Chadbourne stuck his head into the open top of the carrier. "Lieutenant, sounds real bad down there. Want me to make contact?"

Kane nodded. "Yeah. And quick." Then: "Command, can you clarify orders? We have the target in sight, and engagements in progress."

Fucking military chatter. So neutral. Made all of it so easy, the killing, the running away, the "triage" that let the military moles belowground decide who lives, who dies, and when a price is too much to pay.

This mission was about aiding the squads below, securing the city. And now—they just leave? No way. Something happened.

Another wait. Then the voice from the New Pentagon came on again, making no mistake about what Kane was to do.

One of the men in Kane's carrier cleared his throat. Gomez. An old-timer. Seen way more fighting than Kane ever had. Probably looking at less than a year till he was out. A bit of a pension, enough to get somewhere on high ground and hide.

The voice in Kane's ear barked the command. "Lieutenant, you have your orders. Acknowledge compliance and begin carrying them out immediately."

And already Kane was in deep shit. Hesitation. Not what the marines liked. Then, now, or ever. Semper fi—and get your ass moving when we say "move."

But Chadbourne came back. Interesting—he chose not to use the radio to get back to Kane. "Lieutenant, they're screwed down there."

"Tell me. What do you see?"

"Government troops turned on them, then the fucking rebels joined in. And they brought in some heavy artillery. Who knows where that came from."

Kane nodded.

"They're asking for our help as fast as we can get there. My guess is, if we don't hustle, they'll be wiped out real soon."

The earpiece again: "Lieutenant, acknowledge."

Wiped out . . . That's exactly what would happen. There would be no prisoners taken, no prisoner exchange or deals. All evidence of the U. S. of A.'s attempt to "help" the Terekstan government would be erased. Simply the way things worked these days.

"Shit. They got maybe a half hour, Lieutenant. Sounds bad."

Chadbourne kept his eyes on Kane. And though he knew what he should do, Kane could well imagine what was going on in the city below. All of a sudden, you face a force maybe two, three times what you expected, now tightening its noose around you. All evidence erased. The suddenly friendly factions would divide the spoils. And who gets the oil? That deal had probably just been worked out by the dozen lizard lawyers from Moscow and New Washington. Some split worked out, now let's chop up the annoying soldiers who almost screwed the deal.

Kane thought he'd try one thing.

"Command, have you tried negotiating a safe passage for the squads? Bring in some choppers. Get them the hell—"

"Lieutenant, did you not hear the command? You are on another country's sovereign soil. Your role in this mission is now ended. You have responsibility for your own squad and your vehicles. Return to the rally point immediately."

Kane nodded and looked up. Chadbourne had his eyes locked on him. He didn't have to say anything else.

"Orders, Lieutenant?"

"We're going in, Sergeant. Tell everyone it's going to be . . . real fun."

Chadbourne started to turn away.

"Oh—and don't tell them that we've been ordered to turn back."

A grin from Chadbourne. "Yes, sir. It would just . . . confuse them." Then he was gone.

And now, thought Kane, *it's into the meat grinder we go.*

3

IAN KELLIHER TURNED AND LOOKED AT THE SUN, careful not to stare for too long. At a glance, it didn't seem much different from the way the sun looked back home. If anything it looked brighter, clearer, even though Mars was farther away from it.

But the readout on the left arm of his uniform told him it was a crisp 20 degrees below zero outside. A survivable temperature, albeit temporarily, if it was forced upon you. But how long could you last with no air? A few minutes before your brain would scream for oxygen?

There was something he didn't tell the others, about other experiments back home—feeding off work with the free divers who trained their bodies to change their heart rate and metabolism, so that they could hold their breath for eight minutes, or even more. The big secret? With the UAC's chemical modifications and training, that was now up to twenty-six minutes. Now the team was experimenting with the basic components of the Martian atmosphere that was so heavy in carbon dioxide and so poor in oxygen. Could modifications be made so that humans could be on the surface and breathe for *hours* at a time?

Of course, there was still the severe temperature to deal with. Catch a good day, and it could be pleasant. On the other hand, a cold Martian day could freeze your body solid in a matter of minutes. But all that too could be changed. More gases in the atmosphere would trap more of those rays.

Yeah . . . just do what we did to planet Earth. Dump more gas into the atmosphere, and watch the temps climb. And the ice melt. And the coastal areas vanish. And the whole fucking planet change more in a hundred years than it did in the past ten thousand.

We could do that here. In fact, we have to.

But that, Kelliher knew, was quite another story.

"Ian?" Hayden said.

Kelliher turned away from the ridge. He hated that Hayden thought himself a peer, that he'd actually address him by his first name. Made Kelliher a little . . . sick.

"Yes?"

"Ready to see Delta?"

"Not yet. Take me to Site 3."

"Really, sir?" Hayden replied. "You have a lot of

other meetings and briefings this afternoon. And Betruger can meet us now, so don't—"

"Site 3, General Hayden." He waited a beat so that
there could be no mistake about the meaning of the
exchange. "Now, if you will."

Hayden nodded, his eyes looking fishy inside his
helmet.

They walked back to the rover, a nervous Swann
bringing up the rear. And when all loaded, their
driver started to make his serpentine way down the
promontory, curling around to an area of moguls,
small hills, and sharp jutting chunks of red rock that
looked like the tip of a mountain that had jutted up
and through the permafrozen Martian surface.

Kelliher started to get out of the vehicle when he felt
someone tap his shoulder. He turned to see Campbell's hand on it.

"Mr. Kelliher, if you don't mind. I'd like to go first.
Just to take a look . . . for security reasons, sir."

Kelliher nodded, thinking, *That's why I pay him the
big bucks.*

"Be my guest, Jack."

He watched Campbell hop out of the rover and
walk down a makeshift path to what looked like a
massive cave entrance. Explosive charges had widened that opening, and now scaffolding with lights
surrounded it. Two rovers were pulled to the side.

Kelliher watched Campbell walk down to the
opening. Two men stood at the entrance, and Camp-

bell stopped to confer with them. Then the security chief turned and waved at Kelliher and the others.

"General, how many people do you have working down here?" Kelliher asked.

"It varies. We need everybody we can to keep moving on schedule back at Mars City. But the work here—at Site 3—is never quiet."

How about answering the damn question? Kelliher thought. "How many people, Hayden?"

"Um—right now, five. Three working excavation, and two scientists. Lot of people would like to get down here—we've got people even coming down on their own time."

Kelliher walked down the rocky path to the cave entrance until he came abreast of Campbell. "Okay, Jack?"

"Yes, sir. No more explosions for the day. And the others are in there." A beat, then Campbell asked, knowing the answer. "Want to go in, sir?"

"Yeah. I'd like to see for myself."

Campbell turned to one of the sentries, who nodded and, without a command, led the way into the cave.

The massive lights outside lit every corner of the inner walls. And for a few moments, Kelliher didn't see anything more than the smooth surface of Martian rock. Just more red rock . . .

Until, as they got to the edge of the light provided by the array at the cave mouth, he stopped and saw them. Despite thinking there was not much that could really shake him, seeing all this in person certainly did.

Markings. Strange curling symbols. Cut or painted or carved into the rock. First a few, then, with each step, he could see that the walls became filled with them. Symbols. A language? Words?

"Goddamn," Kelliher said slowly.

"Unbelievable," Swann said. Until now, the lawyer had seemed mostly interested in getting his butt back to the lights and air and security of the Administration Wing.

Kelliher heard steps. Two figures loomed out of the darkness ahead, massive lights on top of their EVA suits.

Kelliher turned away from the glare, raising a hand to shield his eyes, and suddenly both lights went off. He turned back to what he now saw were a man and a woman. Two scientists. Geologists perhaps? Language scholars? Or anyone from a half-dozen specialties that would love to be here, to see this?

No matter. It was time to get over the shock and awe of what he was seeing and take control of the situation. "Good morning," Kelliher said in a loud voice. "Allow me to introduce myself. I'm your boss."

After formalities had been exchanged, the woman, Dr. Axelle Graulich, touched one of the carved swirls. Her voice carried a bit of an accent. Kelliher made a note to find out her background—he liked to know . . . everything.

"The dates, well . . . they vary, and carbon dating here is not the exact science we have at home," she was saying. "But we figure . . . they're three hundred . . . maybe four hundred thousand years."

"And that well preserved?" Kelliher asked.

The other scientist, Dr. Tom Stein, spoke up. "The opening had been sealed. So this area was always well protected from the dust storms, the sun . . . the extreme temperatures."

"Any idea what they mean?"

Graulich pulled her hand away from one swirl. She turned and looked at the other array of symbols, the smooth curves giving way to angular lines. *Could they really be letters—or something else?* Kelliher thought. *Maybe—perhaps—a map?*

Graulich shook her head. "We—I mean you, sir— have whole teams back home in Palo Alto working on everything we find. We have also brought the few artifacts we've recovered to Delta. Dr. Betruger, in fact, has been—"

Kelliher turned away, seeing something odd. Swann, who had been invisible for this whole tour, had taken a step forward, touching the swirls of symbols. "'To Serve Man,'" Swann remarked.

"What?" Kelliher said. "What the hell are you talking about?"

Swann turned away from the sheer stone wall.

"Something from two centuries ago, sir. A primitive vid. In the 1950s, there was a vid about a book, an alien language. These scientists decode only the title—at first."

Before Kelliher could ask him what the hell he was talking about, Graulich walked over to the lawyer. "And what happened?" she asked.

Even under his faceplate, Swann looked embarrassed. *So he should be*, Kelliher thought. *Talking about two-hundred-year-old vids, for Christ's sake.*

"They thought it was a good thing, this book from the aliens . . . to serve, to help mankind. People scrambled to visit the alien world, supposedly a garden of Eden."

Graulich raised a hand. "Let me guess. Then they decoded the rest of the book?"

"Exactly."

"And what, Swann," asked Kelliher, quickly losing his patience. "What was the stupid goddamn book?"

Swann turned to his boss. "A cookbook, sir. Turned out it was a cookbook."

Nobody said anything for a second. Then Kelliher began to laugh in spite of his exasperation. It was actually pretty funny. *A cookbook! Of all things.*

And when his laughter subsided, he took a breath. "Okay, this has been . . . most entertaining. Not terribly informative, but definitely entertaining. When either of you do find out something about all this, I want to be the first to know, of course."

"Yes, sir," Graulich said.

He turned to Hayden. "Okay then—let's go visit the star attraction, hmm? Dr. Betruger awaits."

The airlock shut behind them. As soon as he had his helmet off, Kelliher went over to Hayden, addressing him perhaps a little too confrontationally, but then again, time *was* money. "You really think Mars City is going to be completed in time, that you will be able to link Delta Lab with the full complex? In just twelve months?"

Hayden took a deep breath. "Yes. Your office has sent up additional teams, and we have the material we need. The teams are working night and day, no matter what the temperature." Hayden took a breath. "It will get done."

"Good."

Kelliher then noticed Campbell looking at the airlock and the nearby schema showing the layout of the lab.

"Problem, Jack?"

"Sir, this doesn't match what we saw outside."

"What?"

"Look. This layout shows only *one* way into Delta, through the security junction. But then—what's this?"

Hayden went over to check it out for himself. "Oh that? Betruger ordered that. Apparently approved by your design teams on Earth. It's simply an additional point of ingress and egress. A backup, if you will."

"Or an escape route?" Campbell remarked.

"Possibly."

"Did anyone raise the question of security? This lab, doing the most sensitive work, the most important experiments . . . and Betruger orders up a back door?" Campbell shook his head. "I don't get it."

"I suggest you ask Dr. Betruger."

Campbell looked right at Kelliher, "Yeah—I intend to."

4

KANE'S FORCE STOPPED ON A CURVED SECTION of highway, the sides littered with smoking tanks, twisted artillery guns, and what looked like smoldering smudge pots. But from experience, Kane knew that they were bodies. Whether they were civilians or soldiers was anybody's guess.

And now they were close enough to hear the firefight ahead, the surprise noose closing on the other marines.

The acrid smell began to seep into Kane's lead vehicle. Gomez coughed, then said, "Shit." Some of the other grunts began hacking as well.

Kane hit some buttons on the dash, and a holographic floating map of the city appeared in the air. He could touch points to enlarge them, or change the POV, though he didn't need that feature right now.

Chadbourne's voice sounded in his ear. "Lieutenant—any orders?"

"Hold on—I want a live shot of this mess."

Kane scrolled down to access the live sat feed over their position. And then he could see it all. Three groups moving quickly toward a position four, maybe five city blocks away . . . while the marines who were trapped there fired back.

They had—in Kane's estimate—maybe ten or twenty minutes.

"Fuck," Kane grumbled. He pointed to the live enhanced image and began to turn it so he could plot the best way to their position—when the image suddenly vanished.

"What the hell?"

"Lieutenant?"

"Hang on, Chadbourne. Just hold it a second."

The satellite feed had gone completely dead, and, Kane assumed, so had every other bit of live intel that had been fed to his onboard computer. Now they had no eyes, no information. He tried to get back the archived map—that too was gone.

So they were shutting down everything. They'd probably try to kill his battalion's communications system if they didn't already know he had an analog override.

Kane tried to remember the images he saw, the streets, the path taken by the now-allied government and rebel troops repelling the nasty American invaders, who only hours ago had been the city's defenders.

"Okay. All set. We're going to head northwest, then come up on the rear of one of the armies heading straight toward our guys." Classic end-run strategy. "But we can't waste a lot of time when we get there. There are still two other groups moving toward them."

"Exit strategy, Lieutenant?"

Kane wanted to laugh and say, *Just get the hell out.* "We're going to go get to them and open a corridor out."

"Yes, Lieutenant."

And after that? Kane wondered. When they got back to the rally point? Were they still going to get extracted . . . ?

No time to think about that. Even now, they were perhaps left to face an even larger force, some Russians in the mix for good measure, all heading their way.

Or maybe . . . the U.S. in this case would want to clean up its own mess.

A few missile-equipped fighters—that was all it would take.

Whatever. Too late to turn back now. "Okay. Let's go."

Kane stopped the line of armored vehicles. "Break down the column," he commanded, and quickly two of the other vehicles came alongside, leaving just the other two behind.

A voice screeched in his ear. "Where the hell are you?! They got us in a goddamn trap here!"

He would have liked to answer the beleaguered marines, but the less anyone knew about what was coming, the better. Then Chadbourne came on: "Lieutenant, we're running blind here?"

" 'Fraid so, Sergeant. Going to be an old-school operation." Which meant that they had no tech advantage or even parity with the enemy in what was about to happen. It also probably meant that a lot of good men were going to die in this crappy city.

"Okay Sergeant, you carry on straight until you're in contact with the enemy. I'll follow my plan."

An end run. Cutting to the left and then circling back. *If I can remember the layout of this old city.* The curving streets, the dead ends, the roads that narrowed, then led to nothing.

All their vehicles sported twin pulse cannons and each was topped by a rocket launcher. In the old days, these troop carriers would be considered close to tanks.

And the troops? Armed with a mix of plasma guns and machine guns. Kane's squad liked to customize. Everyone was also well equipped with grenades.

Lot of firepower—but would it be enough?

"Show time," Kane said. He looked at his driver, a tight-lipped woman who rarely said anything. Every once in a while he caught her smiling at something one of the squad said.

"McBride," he said to her, "take us right—fast as this thing can go."

She gunned the vehicle, and the others had to

race to follow alongside. Now it all came down to memory.

"Cut left—shit. Hold on."

Kane rubbed his chin, realizing, now that he was in the city proper, how much he needed a map, even the old-fashioned kind. If he wasn't mistaken, one of these roads should loop around to some broad boulevard that looked like it was one of the main arteries being used to wipe out the marines.

He briefly wondered how this story would play out. What would be said? How would the U.S. government explain it to the relatives, the parents, the wives and lovers? No one believed anything the government said anymore . . . about anything. So it almost didn't matter.

"Yeah—okay. Head down there," Kane ordered.

The third armored vehicle had to fall behind as the cobblestoned road quickly narrowed. As Kane watched the progress from the open turret, he started to hear the familiar sounds of endless war—the rapid chugging of machine gun fire, the repetitive dulled booms of rockets exploding inside buildings.

The Terekstan forces were probably knocking the buildings down brick by brick, ready to bury the marines. Kane was painfully aware that he might just be adding his troops to the body count. In which case, Command might have been right to order mission termination.

Fuck it—too late now.

He turned to the twin gunners on top of his vehicle. "Hold your fire until we can see what's happening."

With one voice, the two gunners—in a prime spot
to be taken out—replied, "Yes, Lieutenant."

Kane rubbed his chin again. A nervous habit. Rubbing, thinking. What was ahead? What was the best
way to get the pressure off the trapped marines?

The cobblestone street curved around, then
opened out into a plaza. And ahead he spied the Terekstan troops, and off to the side, the rebels, maybe
even with some Russian regulars thrown in for good
measure, moving down three streets simultaneously,
all nicely coordinated.

Then a rumble, deep, something felt in the gut.
Tanks. Real goddamn tanks, definitely from Mother
Russia . . . unless they were the Chinese knockoffs.

How many soldiers just for this advancing wing
alone? Two . . . maybe three hundred. And probably
an equal number on the other side.

Kane took a breath. Crazy overwhelming odds.
Kane's forty-two soldiers . . . against all that lay before him.

One thing Kane knew for sure—if it turned into
a toe-to-toe battle, fighting for every meter of street,
then the end result was a foregone conclusion: all
the marines would die in this quaint city tonight. Did
the grunts under him know that?

He looked around the armored troop carrier. Faces
grim. Eyes wide. Weapons clutched. Kane thought of

giving them a little rallying speech. But if there was one thing he knew about his marines, it was that their bullshit detectors were set to high.

Still looking at the soldiers, he spoke into the radio mic hugging his cheek. "Sergeant, got the enemy in sight?"

The radio crackled to life, and when Kane heard the gunfire, the explosions, he knew that Chadbourne was doing more than just seeing the enemy.

Kane pointed to the twin side doors of the vehicle. A soldier on each door awaited Kane's move. No speech, no flag waving, no "Semper fi' " or commands like "Leave no marine behind."

Just a single word . . .

"Go!"

The doors popped open; the marines moved out. And all the while Kane was thinking: *We don't have a goddamn chance.*

5

THE AIRLOCK TO DELTA OPENED, AND KELLIHER hurried in ahead of the others. The lock shut behind them and the chamber filled with precious air.

After a few moments, the lock leading to the lab opened, and the party gave their life-support suits to some lab assistants. Kelliher gazed past them, marveling at the sight before him.

The lab past the airlock teemed with activity; people moved through a great open space as if hell-bent on a mission of amazing urgency. Surrounding the great open lab, Kelliher could see chambers and storerooms in the background, and then a raised area, with more rooms.

An incredible display, all of Mars City, all of the UAC's great plans. This lab, its work, the future it represented.

There was, however, one thing missing from Kelliher's sight. "Where the hell is Betruger?"

Swann stood beside his boss. "He was notified that we were on our way."

"Really?"

Despite his irritation, Kelliher knew that Dr. Malcolm Betruger commanded a certain level of respect—he was, after all, the brains behind everything that made the UAC what it was today. And if Betruger was correct about the work up here . . . it was only the beginning.

Nonetheless, Kelliher began to fume. "Am I supposed to stand here and wait? What the—"

Suddenly Betruger came rushing across the floor, emerging from behind a massive podlike chamber on the main floor. "Ian, *so* glad to see you."

Kelliher stuck out his hand. Betruger gave it a quick shake as if such flesh-to-flesh contact bordered on the unappealing.

Physically, Betruger wasn't imposing at all. On the short side, a bit stocky. But the eyes . . . Betruger's eyes burned with an intelligence and clarity that could hold a boardroom riveted, or make every person in the room feel two inches tall, from fellow scientists down to the lowliest lab assistant.

Betruger looked at the other men and nodded, not acknowledging Hayden by name. *Shows who's is in control of this operation.* Kelliher guessed that Betruger certainly liked the fact that Delta was—for now at least—cut off from the rest of Mars City.

"Good to see you again, Malcolm," said Kelliher. "Things look . . . busy here."

A smile, not a terribly warming one, bloomed on Betruger's face. "Busy. Oh yes, that we are, Ian. And it's only going to get more so. You got my requests for the next quarter?"

"Yes, they are being processed—"

Betruger's eyes narrowed. "Processed? Ian, I told you that they represented the minimum. The absolute minimum . . ."

"I still have a board to report to, Malcolm. I'm still on Earth."

A grin from Betruger. "The old world."

"Yes, a magical place where boards still have to sign off on giant budget increases." Though, truth be told, they would rubber stamp any proposal, but why let him know that?

"The minimum, Ian. That's all I—"

Kelliher put a hand on Betruger's shoulder and smiled. "Malcolm, don't worry. It's all going to happen, everything you need. The personnel, the material—I put Swann here in direct charge of overseeing it. He'll be coming up here to liaise with you."

Kelliher saw Swann's head turn at that bit of information. Unexpected news for his chief counsel, but Swann knew a lot of Kelliher's and the UAC's secrets. If there was one person to trust in this, it had to be Swann. And if he didn't like it? *Tough shit, my friend.*

Betruger didn't exactly shrug off the hand on his

shoulder, but instead turned and faced the great open expanse of the lab. "A tour then? Show you where we are . . . and where we will be going?"

Kelliher nodded and smiled. "That's what we're here for, Malcolm. Just nothing too technical, okay?"

"Of course. We'll start with the new chambers, shall we?"

And Betruger hurried away at full speed, making no secret of the fact that he was probably way too busy to be so accommodating.

"Dr. MacDonald, if you would do the honors?"

Kellyn MacDonald turned away from the just-installed chamber, barely put together for this dog and pony show. Certain irony there, he thought. *Dogs. Yes, we've used them. No ponies—yet.*

MacDonald lowered his clipboard and stuck out his hand.

"Ian Kelliher," Betruger said, introducing the UAC boss.

Kelliher took MacDonald's hand, but his eyes were fixed on the twelve-foot-tall, room-sized chamber. "Impressive," he said. Only then did he look at MacDonald. "And untested?"

"Yes, sir. We only—"

Betruger walked up to the chamber. "Not to worry, Ian. It follows the specifications of the smaller modules. We continue to test with those as well. There's no question in my mind that these will be ready for full testing soon, with these pods."

"And operational?"

The question came from a man standing just behind Kelliher. MacDonald looked at him. Strange to see a guy in a suit, on Mars no less. Was this the lawyer he'd heard about? Yes. Elliot Swann, in the flesh. The shark who made sure that no matter what happened on Mars, it didn't come around to bite the UAC. The whole colony could be wiped out in some massive incident and—MacDonald imagined—the UAC not only would be found completely blameless, but would probably come up smelling like roses.

Betruger looked at Swann. "The big question, Elliot. One that—well, I'm sure I need not explain to someone as bright as you—can only be resolved by *testing*."

Was that a bit of a grin on Kelliher's face? Enjoying his lawyer facing Betruger? No one faced Betruger and escaped unscathed. The scientist pushed his glasses back, pausing—a little thinking time. "Just as when I developed the ion engine. That too . . . remained to be *tested*. That *too* spent years without being operational." The scientist took a step closer to the lawyer. *Oh . . . this is fun.* "Until it did become *operational*. Enough to bring you and every person and every bit of machinery and every chunk of Mars City here—in days. Think about that for a moment, Mr. Swann. Days."

Finally General Hayden—who had been lying back as if this lab was a potentially threatening environment—intervened. "All right, Malcolm, I think you've made your point."

Kelliher nodded. "People have questions. I get them all the time. When I go back home, the board will certainly ask them. It's wise to have answers, Malcolm, no? So let's continue the tour. And then maybe I'll have some really good answers for them."

Betruger turned away from the lawyer, and— almost like some barrel-headed clown applying makeup—he plastered a smile on his face. "Yes, Ian. Lots to show you. You'll see everything you need. Follow me."

They turned and walked away. *Everything they need*, MacDonald thought. Maybe. *But they won't see everything.* Of that, MacDonald was absolutely sure.

• • •

Mars City PDA
Dr. Kellyn MacDonald
Personal Folder, Security Enabled.
Checked and Opened_4_27_2144 12:37:42

The "inspection" seems to be progressing exactly as Betruger rehearsed it. Kelliher got to see what he thought was the whole lab—the gleaming new transporter chambers and the older, smaller modules all in working order. While they didn't get a live demonstration, Betruger did show them vid of what he called "key experiments" using physical objects. Then he explained the irregularities, the anomalies—or rather, tried to.

Because we don't know what caused them. Why would the polar orientation of an object's molecules reverse? Why would certain chemical bonds disappear, changing the nature of some substances, while others would be transformed into some new kind of bond, previously unseen?

All fascinating, and why I am here, to be sure. But Betruger, and all of us on the team, made sure that certain things are not seen. All the vid from the live experiments, from example, and the cadavers—kept only a few rooms away from where the party tours. Made me very nervous, I must confess.

Not a single word about that as Betruger plunges on with his experiments, his plans. No one can question him, of course. Heaven forbid—not the man who gave humankind the ion engine. But I am keeping records. And I file my own reports to Kelliher. Then there's my own personal musings here, of course. And copies of files, test results, the images. At some point, I may need to show them. But not right now.

For now, it's watch and wait.

Personal Folder Closed and Locked_4_27_2144 12:51:08

• • •

Betruger walked the tour party back to the airlock. "Satisfied, Ian?"

"Not sure how to answer that, Malcolm. Based on

your test results and what I've seen, there seems to be a lot yet to figure out, a lot—"

"Oh yes—there is, and we will. The team here is the best. You should know—you pay their salaries." Betruger laughed—an unpleasant sound. "But they are all here because each and every one of them believes in what we are doing, what we will attempt."

Kelliher started to step into his EVA suit. "I'm sure they do. I'm sure they understand that if they achieve the goal of moving matter through space instantaneously . . . this dream of teleportation . . ."

"It's not a dream."

Kelliher paused. Betruger was difficult to talk to at the best of times, but there seemed to be an increased edge to his tone. *Is Mars getting to him?* Kelliher looked at Campbell and Swann; both would be dealing hands-on with this man in the coming days and weeks. Good that they see Kelliher's concern. "It is in my book, until you achieve success."

"It's all there. We are so close. Twelve months. At the outer limit."

Kelliher nodded. "I hope so. The UAC has high hopes for Mars City . . ." He grabbed his helmet.

Betruger smiled. "Exactly—everything else pales. And when I succeed, humanity will be forever changed."

"I'm sure. And now—thanks again, but General Hayden has some boring administrative matters I have to review."

Kelliher was about to reach out and shake the lead scientist's hand, but stopped himself. Somehow, it just didn't feel like something he wanted to do. His instincts warned him that something was completely *off* about the entire situation up here.

6

THE INNER CITY OF TEREKSTAN

WITHOUT WARNING, KANE'S SQUAD FOUND THEMselves right on the tail of a line of Terekstan regulars, flanking some nasty Russian tanks. The tanks were relics, nothing more than turrets with wheels, but still capable of kicking out rapid-fire explosive rounds without jamming.

The gunfire covered Kane's advance, coming right behind them. The Terekstan soldiers were too busy watching their tanks turn buildings into rubble, and apparently Russia hadn't given them any live satellite feeds. Maybe they didn't think it necessary. And judging from the building-leveling blasts, Kane imagined that they weren't too concerned about rebuilding any infrastructure.

"Chadbourne, what do you see?"

"Nothing yet, Lieutenant. Just signs of the firefight ahead."

Then another voice. One of the trapped marines. "Th-they got us surrounded. We're just about out of RPGs. They're pounding us."

Kane saw a few of the Terekstan soldiers ahead turn their heads, now suddenly aware that someone snaked behind them.

"Shit," he called out. "Everyone ready."

And just like that, the Terekstan soldiers who had been pouring all of their firepower into the buildings began to aim at Kane's men.

"Deploy and fire at will!" Kane shouted.

The sides of the troop carriers opened, and his men streamed out, hugging the building walls.

The area immediately transformed into a massive firefight, a spidery net of tracer fire and laser targeting, making the crater-pocked boulevard look like a carnival setting. Or maybe a street from hell.

The Terekstan regulars in the rear—easy targets—began to fall. *Good. When you're this outnumbered, you have to start whittling them down fast.*

"Lieutenant, we have a problem," reported Chadbourne.

"Which one?"

"They've moved to the side streets and taken position. We—" He hesitated. Kane could hear the sound of guns firing, then larger explosions. God, maybe this was an error. What's the expression? Good after bad? *What if this rescue turns out to be a mass slaughter of two companies?*

"Chadbourne, maybe you need to pull back."

No response. Then—"No, Lieutenant. We've taken position." A laugh. "One thing for sure. We got plenty of targets." *If there's anyone I want coming to rescue me, it's Chadbourne.*

Then the trapped marine's voice again, the one that had totally lost it before. "Lieutenant—if you can hear me—how long till you're here?"

"Are you the officer in charge?"

"The captain, he's dead. I just put on his headset."

"Good work. Your marines in defensive position?"

"Yes—but more than half gone."

Cuts our number down even more . . . "We're real close. What's your name?"

"PFC Richards."

"Richards, you're doing great. Real good. Just keep the pressure on at your end. Once we see your position, once we—" A loud explosion near Kane's vehicle—he felt it lurch as the driver drew closer to a building. "Once we see your position, we'll send up some flares. That will be your signal to punch out and join us."

"Yes, Lieutenant."

"Meantime—just keep firing."

Give them, what, five minutes? Kane wondered. He turned back to the driver. "Do your best to keep those goddamn tanks busy. Got it?" His two gunners nodded. Both looked a little jittery . . .

And then Kane jumped out of the vehicle to join his men on the street. *This must have been what Custer felt like.*

The Terekstan tanks, either bought, borrowed, or stolen from the Russians, finally had time to position themselves and seal off the end of the street. At the same time, snipers had taken position in the buildings at the corners.

They could pin us down here forever, Kane knew. *Or worse, one of the other enemy lines moving down a parallel street could turn around and box us in at the other end. Game over.*

He turned to one of the lead soldiers. "Okay, Jackson—we got to get into those buildings and take out the snipers. Take the right building—" The head of the man standing beside Jackson exploded, spraying Kane and Jackson with blood and bone. "Better get moving, Jackson," Kane said without missing a beat.

And the soldier took off.

A quick glance to see that the rest of his men were still in place. Good. Nobody backing away a few meters after that grisly display—everyone standing their ground.

He caught the eye of another grunt and pointed at the building to the right that Jackson had just entered. "You, too. Go!"

More explosions—and talking was useless. But Kane did some quick jabs in the air, telling another group of marines to start moving, signaling that they were to follow him. The rest kept up the street-level firefight. While armored support kept trading blasts with the tanks, the two groups entered the nearby buildings.

Kane led his men upstairs, crossing places where the steps ended at a giant hole, a chunk of staircase to nowhere suspended in the air like something from a nightmare. Outside he could hear the whistling of the gunfire, the exploding shells.

He had minutes, if that. The goal was to get to the roof and head down to face those corner buildings, because those snipers had to go.

They reached the top landing, and Kane spotted two men—not in Terekstan uniforms—racing toward him. Without aiming, he fired his weapon, the two men collapsing in front of him.

They were probably guerrillas or civilian conscripts sent to stop his squad, meaning someone had figured out what they were up to. No matter. There was no Plan B. It was this, or obliteration.

At the end of the top floor hallway he came to a wide metal door blocking the way to the roof. "Blow it," he ordered to the soldier behind him, who wasted no time in attaching a small thermal charge. Kane and the others turned away and backed up a few steps.

In seconds, the dark hallway was filled with glowing light, then pungent bluish smoke. And even before the smoke cleared, Kane led his squad forward.

He just hoped Jackson was moving as quickly. The man used to play football. *Hope he still has his legs.*

On the other hand, they could have run into some bad luck and already be lying dead in the other building.

While Kane moved forward, he spoke to his vehicles below. "Okay, start moving—"

"But, Lieutenant—"

"I said *move*. As fast as you can." Then: "Chadbourne? Where are you?"

"Almost there, Lieutenant. Christ, they have a lot of men on the ground, and in those buildings—and man, so many of those T-90 Tigers."

"Just keep the pressure on. We'll be at the target zone in two minutes." *If we make it . . .*

Kane bolted forward, knowing that his men would hustle to move at his speed. He raised his weapon to hip level, and then pulled out his plasma gun. Hopefully every grunt behind him was doing the same.

Grenades dangled off every spare place on his belt and shoulder straps. With protective vests that could absorb some direct hits, they were about as good shape for causing maximum damage as a modern foot soldier could be.

He spied a line of figures at the other end of the roof; more Terekstan regulars spinning around from their sniping positions.

Kane wasted no time, using his two weapons to shoot a spray of firepower out, and—a brief pause— he made a big open T with his arms, indicating that all the men with him should go to either side of him. And he closed that T, his weapons again facing front, firing blast after blast.

All his men needed to see, to hear, was their lieutenant out front, firing full out. And of course, then everyone knew what to do.

Kane wheeled behind a brick chimney that had been blasted into a jagged stump. Not much cover, but it was something.

More enemies kept pouring out of a staircase ahead like some military clown car from the circus. The soldiers Kane was attempting to rescue had only minutes before they'd be completely surrounded and wiped out.

Kane unclipped two grenades. He hit the auto-timer in each—a preset five seconds—and tossed them.

He counted in his head as he saw the first soldiers look at the rolling explosives.

Five. Four.

The lead enemy soldiers split to the side, and Kane saw fire from behind him take them out. Nice work . . .

Three. Two.

Another group of new arrivals emerged onto the far roof. They looked down at the explosives. Only a fatal second to decide what to do.

One.

Except a second wasn't nearly enough time. Like

a perfect golf shot, the two grenades had rolled right next to the opening.

Zero.

The roof opening erupted into a fiery blast and sent a great belch of gray smoke into the night sky.

Kane looked back to the men behind him. All it took was a tilt of his head, and they started forward again, running now toward the still smoking end of the building.

He gestured at three of them, then shouted, "Stay here. Lay down some cover for us." He looked at the smoky stairwell. "The rest of you—let's hope there are still some stairs left."

With the snipers gone, Kane's armored vehicles had also been able to move forward, now protected from above, facing only the forces in front. Which was plenty.

Kane found a recessed doorway and ducked into it. "Chadbourne—you almost here?"

"Got your back, Lieutenant."

Then Kane could see Chadbourne leading his group, firing, hugging the buildings, making damn good progress.

Except that there was this side street. More of a lane, a narrow cobblestoned path that curved away from the open plaza. *I must have missed it on the map*, Kane thought. Just a squiggle. But now filled with a line of soldiers, with a perfect opportunity to surprise Chadbourne's group.

The marines giving his guys cover on top wouldn't see them at all—the buildings shielded them.

Kane turned back to his squad. "See them? We have to take those bastards out now."

Which meant that they'd have to move forward, ignoring their main target, the ring of Terekstan soldiers tightening their grip around the trapped marines. *Not a good situation,* Kane thought. *But either way, it will all be over in minutes . . .*

7

JACK CAMPBELL SHUT THE DOOR TO THE MAIN conference room as Ian Kelliher sat down at the head of the polished mahogany table. As for Swann—for a moment the lawyer looked like he didn't know which of the ten empty chairs to take.

"Damn it, just sit *anywhere*, Swann. You're making me jumpy," Kelliher remarked.

Swann took a seat on the side.

"Mr. Kelliher," Campbell said, "would you like the blinds closed?"

Kelliher looked out the windows, watching people walking back and forth, glancing into the big room.

"Not yet. Wait till Hayden gets back. Let these people see who the hell they're working for." After a few moments, he turned to Swann. "Okay, before

Hayden gets here, let's review the way things will go in the next year."

Swann slipped out his PDA, and immediately Kelliher rolled his eyes.

"No, Christ, I don't want any record of this conversation. Just your ears, Swann, got it? Campbell can remind you of anything you forget."

"Mr. Kelliher," Swann said, "are you sure you don't want to wait until we get back to Earth? I mean—" he looked around at the conference room—"who knows what kind of devices they have in here?"

Campbell took a step away from the door. "I do. My guys went over this room. It is, as Hayden assured us, secure." He nodded at Kelliher. "You can speak freely."

"Okay. Here's what worries me. I don't think Betruger is showing or telling us everything."

"But why would he hide—?" Swann began.

Kelliher laughed. "Swann, for a great lawyer, you tend to be pretty gullible. I *know* Betruger. Even when he was working on the ion engine, I believed only half his promises."

"But that turned out to be exactly as he said."

"Not exactly. The upper limits kept coming down; his claim that it might be modified for short-range use—all that went out the window. But—and it's a big 'but'—he still did something that transformed interplanetary space travel."

Kelliher glanced out the window at the two marines standing outside.

The door opened and General Hayden walked in. "Sorry—wanted to make sure we had everything ready for you."

"Good. Okay, Campbell—now you can shut the blinds and let's get this going."

The security chief tapped a button on a nearby console, and the clear windows immediately turned opaque.

"There they go . . ." Private Maria Moraetes watched the glass of the conference room window turn from clear to a silky white, showing nothing of what was on the other side.

"Some secret stuff going down now," the other marine, Rodriguez, remarked.

"Yeah," said Moraetes. "I guess so."

Rodriguez was just another empty-headed grunt, with a tendency to laugh at absolutely nothing. *Just great*, thought Moraetes. *My first week up here, and because I'm Cuban, they team me up with this idiot. Just because our last names have a lot of vowels. Some things never change.*

"So we just stand out here," she said. "Guarding?"

"Guess so. Guarding what . . . from what? I don't know. Beats EVA patrol, though. Wait till you do that. Gets so damn creepy, especially at night. You almost start thinking you see things out there."

"I bet."

Workers hurried past them at top speed, every department probably ordered by the general to make this place look like one bustling hive of activity.

And she had to wonder: was this a good decision? She could have stayed a marine on Earth, doing administrative work, data management, or any of the desk-related jobs offered. Not much there that seemed like the duties of a space marine, though. This, at least, was a completely different environment than anything she'd ever experienced—even if all she was doing was standing around, a plasma rifle slung over her shoulder, guarding a conference room.

Rodriguez leaned closer. "Hey, Maria, when our shift is done, we could hang in the rec room. You know, just—"

She glared at him. "No. I *don't* know. And I have a lot of reading up to do. I'm supposed to have the completed Mars City layout memorized within two weeks."

Rodriguez laughed. "Look, they won't have this place done for another twelve months, if that. Don't worry about it. But suit yourself. I'm just being friendly."

"Thanks." As in, *No thanks.* She turned to the conference room. "Wish I could be a fly on the wall in there."

His weird smile returned. "Oh yeah, there's lots of things about this place they don't want us knowing about. Things happening." His grin widened. "Maybe we could talk about it sometime. But you didn't seem interested."

She nodded. Maybe that wasn't such a bad idea after all, even if the information came from this idiot. Something told her that the more she knew about Mars City, the better.

"MacDonald—come here."

The scientist looked up from his keyboard, well used to Betruger snapping orders at him, treating him like some kind of lab assistant.

Back on Earth, in a still calm and quiet part of California, close to the Sierra mountains, his family went on with their lives, speaking to him daily, his wife sharing the little moments in their two children's lives. His son Patrick, nearly five, already playing soccer . . . his daughter Samantha's birthday party coming soon, complete with giant cake, balloons, and, and—

Why the hell am I missing that?

He thought he knew the answer to that question. The opportunity to work with the great Dr. Malcolm Betruger and his handpicked team on this . . . technology . . . that could change everything. At the time, it didn't seem like the word no was even a possibility.

At the time . . .

Even his wife had insisted that he had to do it. All MacDonald's work, in the major research facilities of Cal Tech, MIT, RPI—it all led to this. From those first breakthroughs of the previous century, where electrons were beamed through space, to the actual reconstruction of atoms, moved from one location to another.

Instantly.

It bordered on the incredible, the implications nothing short of amazing.

And Betruger, the creator of the ion engine, was soon getting any and all funding to pursue this dream. There were rumors of amazing breakthroughs. And finally MacDonald knew that any personal work he might undertake in this area was meaningless, if he wasn't part of Betruger's team.

But what did that mean? It meant signing on as a good soldier working under the great one himself. Taking orders. Following commands. Not at all what MacDonald imagined it would be.

He had tried to convince his wife Ann to come to Mars City. But she wanted a normal life for herself and the kids. Grass instead of reddish dirt. Clean cool mountain breezes instead of a helmet with compressed air. A summer's night when the setting sun turned the sky a deep, lush orange before sinking and the pale blue deepened into an indescribable indigo.

"No," she had said in a way that made it clear that there was no debate. "You, on the other hand, *have* to go. It's everything you've always dreamed about. Do this amazing work, and come back when you can. We can see you and talk every day." He knew that she would miss him terribly. But it said something about her love that she insisted that he do this.

Now, though working here, he wondered if it was all worth it. To say that his relationship with Betruger had grown frosty was an understatement.

Betruger now stood close to one of the new full-sized chambers. They had just gotten them out on the floor simply for display. The show for the visiting brass.

"Yes, Malcolm?" *I should call him Betruger,* MacDonald thought. *Show him the same lack of respect he shows me.*

"I think we should move these new pods into operational mode as quickly as possible."

Betruger touched the smooth surface of the pod, an inch and a half of advanced clear polymer. One could explode a bomb inside the chamber, and the shell would still hold.

"You think that's a good idea?"

Betruger turned to him. "I am asking you what *you* think. You have been overseeing their preparation. I mean, these have been built to specifications you have been working on for months, no?"

MacDonald tried hard not to answer in kind. "Right. That's true. And my schedule has them remaining offline for at least two, maybe three months. We need to do additional work with the small chambers. We still don't have any hypotheses to explain—"

Betruger shook his head. "Explain? That's what you want? Explanations? Answers? Here are, pushing into a new technology where answers, any explanation, might be difficult if not impossible to find. And you would hold up everything—just for that?"

MacDonald waited a few seconds. A technique he had picked up since arriving on Mars. Don't snap at the bait. He'd seen other scientists get into arguments with Betruger, then watched them get chewed to bits. Some associates had quit, and more than a few had been openly dismissed.

And new ones showed up in their place—all loyal and unquestioning, all forming a protective ring around Betruger.

And here—

And here . . . MacDonald came to the real reason he stayed, the real reason he would continue this work. Someone had to see, to watch, to monitor. Not just to send images and reports to Kelliher.

When MacDonald had enough evidence, he could go to—

Well, to whom, anyway? That could be determined later. Not just Kelliher, though. It was important that MacDonald stay here. And not necessarily for the future of the teleportation project, but for the bigger picture as well.

"Let me just say, Malcolm . . . we aren't ready to make these operational. So, I wouldn't advise using them."

Betruger nodded. "So then, what *would* you advise?"

MacDonald instinctively glanced at the massive

locked storage room, essentially a minilab within Delta, in the rear. The tour hadn't wandered over there. Good thing, too.

"I think we need more experiments with inanimate and animate objects, using the smaller chambers. Give us some time to analyze the changes, the aberrations—"

Betruger shook his head like a scolding parent who didn't buy into the excuse. MacDonald knew he had to give the project director something more. "And then, we can start major experiments with these full-sized chambers, knowing what to look for, and analyze the source of any discrepancies. . . . It would just be a matter of months."

Betruger's bullet-shaped head nodded. His lips tightly pursed. He was about to say something, quite possibly even telling MacDonald to catch the next shuttle back to Earth.

But then the head scientist took a breath and sighed. "Very well. We will stick to the planned itinerary. For now. But I want some tests this evening. *After* our guests have left. Alert the full team. Normal security for the area. Make sure Hayden knows."

Another of MacDonald's tasks—passing on Betruger's will to the full team of scientists.

Not for the first time, MacDonald thought, *This is more of a military operation than a scientific research project. Orders, chain of command, and a crazed race to the finish line driven by fear or who knows what.*

"Okay, no problem."

"Good. And MacDonald—tonight we will attempt a repeat of last Thursday's experiment. Understand?"

Last Thursday. A night to remember, MacDonald thought. Rather, a night to haunt the dark hours of sleep.

"Yes. I'll make sure everything—and everyone—is ready."

8

THE INNER CITY OF TEREKSTAN

KANE LOOKED AT THE STREAMING COLUMN OF soldiers about to cut into Chadbourne's line. He looked left to see if Jackson and the soldiers on the right flank were making their way off the roof and down to the street.

Not yet—which meant it fell to Kane to try and stop what was about to happen. He tried yelling into the radio: "Sergeant! Freeze! Don't move—"

The radio earpiece crackled to life, but the noise from the fire being laid down by Chadbourne's men made the words a hopeless garble. The warning was lost.

To Kane's left, the Terekstan regulars kept firing at their location, nearly pinning them, while Chadbourne steadily walked into a trap. He wouldn't see that winding street up to the right until it was too late.

Kane knew he had no choice. It was either move now, or let this whole operation go south.

He turned back to the solders hugging the stone walls near him, spraying bullets toward the open corridor, firing the occasional RPG to make the enemy back off.

With time, Kane might have been able to let the fight just play out like this until they had a good sense of where the enemy had positioned his troops. But blasts from their small, compact tanks were ripping out chunks of the corner buildings. *Our cover is slipping away . . .*

He thought of times other officers had given orders like the one he was about to issue. To move, even though you knew that at least half of your soldiers would be obliterated.

But there was no alternative. Every second, the danger grew worse, and Chadbourne's entire column was about to be wiped out.

Kane turned to the soldiers behind him. They already figured what was coming. Experienced from countless skirmishes around the world, Kane knew they could read his mind.

The armored vehicles beside them kept blasting away.

He gave the command—one AAV to head left, right into the mouth of the open square, giving some cover to the squad, while the other AAV and its ground troops followed Kane to intersect Chadbourne's column before it was too late.

A few nods. A barely heard "Roger, Lieutenant" from the armored vehicle drivers. Then: "Okay, let's go!"

And there was no looking back for anyone.

Kane had no idea how the left wing was doing. Hopefully they'd soon be joined by the second roof-top party, spilling out onto the square. With luck they could take out the tanks with some heavy explosives and force any ground soldiers and snipers well back.

And if they got that far, Kane could order the sur-rounded force to punch out of their hole . . . then get the hell out of here.

Kane kept leading his men forward, ducking a hail of gunfire, dodging RPGs that seemed—amazing-ly—to just miss his soldiers. He turned and spotted Cammie, as kickass a soldier as he'd ever seen, tak-ing the lead. She had a taste for this—losing all fear, maybe never even having any to begin with. Her gun turning white-hot in her hands, blasting at the enemy.

Amazing shooting. She paused only to lob a gre-nade or two. Then he saw a red dot bloom on her forehead and she fell forward, her finger still tight around the trigger.

Lot of good people are going to fall here. He heard the stinging whine of a bullet zipping past his head. *Too close. Almost had my name on it.*

The enemy across the courtyard had spotted their move and probably guessed that they were heading to spoil the ambush. But Kane had gotten his troops

in good position to force them back and give Chadbourne cover.

Without warning, Chadbourne's solders and vehicles came rushing forward, racing to what they
saw was the main action ahead, to where trapped
marines waited to be rescued.

Kane looked back and pointed ahead, signaling
that everyone had to move now—and fast.

But he could see it was too late.

A flurry of rocket grenades hit the first of Chadbourne's AAVs, then the second, creating massive
blasts that even from a distance nearly blew Kane off
his feet.

Chadbourne and his men stood exposed. They
started scrambling for cover, but the nearest refuge
was across the plaza, back where Kane had come
from . . .

And now the perfectly positioned enemy line
appeared and started mowing down Chadbourne's
troops. Some were riddled by machine gun fire, others vaporized into craters on the street thanks to the
powerful RPGs.

No, Kane thought. *Don't let this happen. Don't let—*

He was close enough to see Chadbourne now, see
his teeth set, eyes ahead, looking for some way out
of this goddamn trap. But even with Kane and his
solders trying to provide cover, taking shots, drawing
fire, there was no way out.

Something hit Chadbourne—a rocket grenade?
Some hyper-charged pulse rifle? Or something else?

Chadbourne had just turned back, maybe to see how many soldiers he had left. Maybe he caught a quick look at Kane trying to help. But then—Chadbourne literally exploded, his body a reddish cloud erupting on the ancient cobblestoned street.

Immediately Kane realized two things: he had failed to protect his own marines, and now he had to get his troops behind him into position to somehow try to get those trapped marines out, all without proper backup.

Because that's what this was all about, wasn't it? A rescue mission—get them out?

He was no longer certain about anything.

Kane ordered his troops to move left—and see if anything could be salvaged out of what he now knew was an absolute clusterfuck about to get even worse.

Jackson and the marines from the right, just down from their own rooftop nightmare, fell into line behind Kane's group. A quick glance told him some good people had fallen.

No time to dwell on any of that. He heard voices and the sounds of fire from just ahead. They had almost reached the building with the trapped marines. Showtime.

"Private Richards? You hear me in there? Time to link up. Get your men moving now!"

"Yes, Lieutenant. But there's still a lot of fire—"

"Move *now*, Private."

A heavy explosion—the Terekstan regulars peppering the area with RPGs.

"Y-yes, Lieutenant. Moving out now."

"Good. We'll do our best—"

Another explosion, bigger this time.

"—to keep this hole opened."

Though Kane's soldiers had arranged themselves in a phalanx formation, using the walls and still-smoking tanks as cover, the situation was anything but good. All too easy to have the trap close on them as well.

There was no need to give any orders; his people picked their targets of opportunity, kept pumping out rounds, in full battle mode—fighting for their lives as well as their fellow marines standing beside them.

Come on, come on, Kane thought.

Every second let the enemy move a little closer, try to plug that hole, tighten the goddamn trap so now it encircled *both* groups of marines.

But then, somehow, through the smoky haze of a thousand rounds and dozens of rocket explosions, the trapped marines streamed out.

And with them in sight, it was time to get the hell out of here.

What would the textbooks call it? A fighting retreat. A maneuver as old as war itself, from the Greeks all the way down to the failed wars of the last century, and ultimately to this mess. The idea of simply shooting as much as you could while getting your ass out in one piece as fast as you could.

Kane saw the trapped soldiers, some firing as they ran to join up, others just full-on running, hungry, possibly even starving, and God knew what their water situation was. . . .

Kane's armored vehicles—the only two still operational—had pivoted and started zipping a line of fire around the buildings, creating just enough mayhem so that the new arrivals could join up with Kane's force.

One jarhead with a sooty face, eyes bugging out of his head, teeth looking ghoulish in his blackened visage, came up to Kane. "That's it, sir—everybody's out."

This had to be the private whom Kane had been talking to all along. "Good work, Richards." Their force had now doubled in size, but who knew how much fight was left in them?

The marines continued to be hammered by the never-ending fire, some falling onto the cobblestoned street. His surviving medics tried to get to them—if a jarhead was still breathing, there was no way they'd be left behind.

"Okay, let's double-time—"

Zip . . .

A bullet cut into Kane's shoulder, like someone had taken a knife to the soft skin behind the shoulder blade. The bullet had found a small spot where his armored jacket gave him no protection. Dammit!

"Move!" he yelled through the pain.

And the two groups, now intermingled, started

hustling out of the plaza, back to the street, the AAVs now behind them, moving as fast as they could. Because they all knew that if the Terekstan troops closed the opening at the other end of the long street, it was game over.

Kane ignored the blood now seeping under his armored jacket and coating his skin; he could feel the material of his fatigues rubbing against the open wound, making it worse. But he had to keep moving—after all, this was his show. His *call*.

He was the one who had ignored orders. Now, as a result, dozens of marines lay dead, a pair of high-tech AAVs were trashed, and they still weren't out of this hellhole of a city.

He kept looking up to make sure that the other end of the street remained clear, that they still had a shot to get across the river. The Terekstan troops could follow, but he'd have a good position from which to push back at them. At least that was the plan.

As the AAVs brought up the rear, Kane saw that the gunners were laying down as much covering fire behind the group as possible.

All of a sudden, it looked like this plan might in fact be working. The cost had been high, but for the thirty marines rescued, it was worth it.

He looked back at the rear, the smoking, burning inner city falling behind. Dammit—it was *working!*

Dark figures quickly filled the street at the other

end. Some crouched—setting up rocket launchers, no doubt—while others began filing down the street, hugging the dark building walls—closing off their only exit and sealing it tight.

So it had come to this: there was absolutely nothing more to be done, nothing but to keep going, driving forward. Kane imagined that every marine felt his stomach tighten. Every marine mentally calculated how much ammo they had, how many grenades, how many able bodies remained to fire back and give them some chance of getting out.

Even Kane had to admit the odds didn't look very good at all.

9

KELLIHER LOOKED AROUND THE LARGE CONFER-
ence room. Everyone in attendance was now hidden from everyone outside. He glared at Hayden,
who—he imagined—knew what was coming.

"I know about the experiments . . ." Kelliher said
quietly.

Hayden looked at Campbell and Swann as if wondering if they were as confused as he was. *Or as confused as he was pretending to be . . .*

"What do you mean, Ian? The work that's been
going on, everything Betruger has been—"

Kelliher put up a hand. "No. Not that little show
we saw today. Everything looking so good, proceed-
ing according to plan. When the truth is . . . well . . .
something else, right?"

Several emotions played across Hayden's face, and

Kelliher wondered if the general would try to deny the truth or give in and accept that Kelliher already knew what was really going on in the lab.

"Mr. Kelliher," Swann added, "perhaps you want to mention to General Hayden about our liabilities, our exposure—"

"In good time," Kelliher said. "There are more important things to discuss now."

Hayden cleared his throat. "You obviously know something that we need to talk about."

"Exactly. The smaller chambers that Betruger has been using . . . his tests with *animate* objects—live specimens . . . they have not gone well, have they?"

Hayden hesitated, as if considering a lie. Then: "There have been—what does he call them?—anomalies. All to be expected, he has explained."

"Expected? And yet you and he saw fit to keep those results from me. In fact, you have done everything possible to make sure that no one outside of Delta knew about any of those experiments."

Hayden nodded. "Yes. That's true."

"And why is that?"

"They were too disturbing, too alarming, Betruger said. I myself haven't seen much. But Dr. Betruger felt that the impact back on Earth, back at the UAC offices, could hurt the project."

"And so the security lid was tightened?"

"It was the only way he could—"

Kelliher turned away and spoke to Campbell. "Show him, Jack."

The room's lighting fell to a pale blue glow and the wall behind Kelliher turned into a screen. Campbell had his PDA out and sent the first 3-D image to the room's display system.

It was a little gray mouse. Except the rear of its body tapered off into what looked like a chunk of segmented worm, or a snake, hairless, thick—

"Nice, huh? Next."

The mouse vanished, to be replaced with what looked like a cat. This vid moved in a loop, showing the cat moving, twisting.

"I've kept the sound off. It's a little much for my stomach."

Kelliher was sure that nobody wanted sound, not when they saw the cat's head opening and shutting like a clamshell rimmed with teeth. The only clue that the mouth of teeth belonged to something feline was the whiskers that sprouted around the gaping mouth.

"There is a second part to this vid where it begins gnawing at its own body. We'll pass that one up, I think."

In the pale blue light he saw Hayden turn away.

"You've seen these before, right?"

Hayden nodded. "Some. I—"

"One more. Just so we know exactly what we are talking about—"

A new image flashed on the screen.

"God," Swann muttered.

Kelliher looked at the screen. Would Swann start gagging? That wasn't entirely out of the question.

• • •

Private James Walker, on break from his security detail inside Delta, sat alone in the cafeteria. On his tray were soy patties shaped to resemble sliced beef, covered in a thick dark gravy, with imitation potatoes and corn to the side.

He held the fork in his hand, ready to scoop up some of the food. But his hand remained poised, as if taking that first stabbing plunge were a momentous decision.

He didn't always eat alone. He used to sit with the others.

But when he realized that he had nothing to say, when he saw the others looking at him, wondering why he was so quiet, why he was acting so strange, he started sitting by himself.

It was better like this.

Better for thinking. Better for planning.

Sleep had grown ever more elusive. Most nights he spent hours tossing and turning. And then, of course, when he did fall asleep, the nightmares came, the parade of things that he had only glimpsed in the lab.

Only, in the nightmares, it didn't end there.

No, the creatures from the lab were only the beginning of the parade, as other things marched out of the chambers and slithered, chewed—things that no longer had any resemblance to the animals that had been used for the experiment.

And, in the nightmare, they would see him.

The ones with eyes, that is. Look at him, trying to corner him, until he knew—absolutely knew—that they would feed on him.

Most evenings, that's how the nightmare went.

But then—

—on *other* nights, something different happened. Something filled the lab—a reddish light, an energy, touching everyone inside it. And Walker could see the other guards and the scientists, all changing, and their mouths opened and shut in some dull mimicry of the nightmare creatures.

They were hungry.

Then the realization . . .

I am hungry—and I will never be satiated.

And Walker would wake up screaming, begging for help, shouting the words, babbling, "No, God, no . . . please no . . ."

Until the room came back into focus. The darkened bunks, now filled with other marines telling him to shut the hell up, we're trying to sleep here.

And one would think that they would be mad at him. But he wasn't alone. Others did exactly the same thing. Though commanders would shift them around to different quarters, there were always a few more.

Most of them probably had the exact same thought: *I have to get out of here. Before I go completely insane.*

Unless . . .

Unless . . .

I already am.

Walker's eyes looked left and right, checking whether anyone was looking at at him, studying him as he sat there, thinking, planning . . .

But no.

No one seemed to be watching.

He let his fork plunge down into the gravy volcano of the potatoes, already cold.

"Hey, Axelle—over here."

Dr. Axelle Graulich had been carefully working on a small section of the wall, slowly brushing away the red stone, trying to uncover as much of the detail below as possible.

Delicate and tedious work. But the reward would be huge—a full section of this wall and the carvings underneath would be exposed. And then—perhaps deciphered.

The very idea made her heart beat fast. To read and understand something from perhaps aeons ago, from the dawn of Martian history, when other intelligent organisms were here.

Except, there were a few curious things . . .

For example, how come they hadn't found any traces of those organisms? No fossils, no organic material—at least, not in the areas they had dug into so far.

Graulich knew that they had only scratched the surface. With most of Mars permanently frozen just a foot below the ground, not much excavation had been done at all. But this cave was an incredible opportunity. She was thankful for UAC's support of this work. Of course, they probably imagined there would be something for them to exploit.

No matter. That's what Mars City, this whole base, was about, wasn't it?

Except for the rumors she heard.

She turned to the voice—Tom Stein, a young but talented paleobiologist with a lot of geology training as well. He was a bit overeager but knowledgeable. He had been working with an advance team, probing the depths of the cave. Graulich got up and walked into the dark of the cave.

"What's up, Tom?"

A few assistants had used pneumatic picks and hammers to clear away a pile of rubble. "Look at this. *This* is interesting." He pointed toward where there had once been a smooth pile of giant red stone.

"You're making good progress—that's great."

"No. That's not it." She was close enough to hear Tom's voice echoing from inside his helmet. "See—we thought this was some kind of rock fall. Like"—he pointed his light to the cave ceiling above them—"from there. But that's impossible. I mean, the geology guys said there are no signs of a major collapse."

Graulich let her lamp point at the cave ceiling. And it was true—there were no signs of anything having plummeted to the ground, no massive gouges, no indentations, no holes.

"So, this didn't fall from up there?"

"Right." Under his faceplate Stein smiled. "So how'd it get here? What happened?"

"I assume your geology team is working on that . . ."

Stein shook his head. "No way. I mean, they're doing analysis of the rock all right. But I think we have the answer already. Guys, hold up a minute." His assistants stopped their work.

Stein tilted his head, signaling that Graulich should follow him. "Careful—some nasty edges."

Graulich clambered on top of a large rock and followed Stein, being careful not to let her boots slide into a crevasse and get trapped, looking for a perch, and then at spots even scrambling on all fours. Until they reached what looked like a hole.

"Teddy here noticed this yesterday."

"Noticed what?"

Stein's grin widened under his helmet. "This. Look."

He opened his fist, and Graulich could see that he had a handful of red dirt. "Observe—" he said with glee. He let a thin trail of dirt trickle down into the hole . . . and the tiny dust-sized particles blew back *up*. A thin red stream of Martian dust . . . being blown away.

"Wow. You mean—"

Stein stood up. "It's a hole, Axelle. It goes somewhere, where there are drafts, some currents of air, winds strong enough to blow this dust back. This cave entrance is only just that—an entrance. This"—he pointed at the small opening—"goes somewhere."

Then Axelle looked at the jumble of rocks that they stood on.

"Yeah. And these rocks?" Stein continued. "These rocks didn't fall 'from' anywhere. My guess is that they were . . . put here."

"Put here?"

"To seal this off. And now, millions of years later, we're going to open it. Pretty cool, hmm?"

Axelle nodded. Though she wasn't sure *cool* was the word she'd use. She turned and looked out at the cave mouth, a giant opening where she could see a curved slice of Martian terrain, hills in the distance, a bit of the unfinished Delta Labs, the Martian sky burning with its usual afternoon intensity.

And as if in a reflex, she backed away from the hole, taking care not to fall, as she started thinking about the implications of this discovery, not quite knowing where to begin.

10

TEREKSTAN—THE BRIDGE ROAD

KANE'S TECH NCO CAME UP TO HIM. "STILL NO signal, Lieutenant."

"Thanks, Gonzales. Best pack up your radio and put a gun in both hands."

"Will do, Lieutenant."

This was probably more than Gonzales bargained for—a kid from some crappy area who got a bit of tech training, then signed on to the Corps thinking that the marines, for him, would be all about keeping a smooth flow of images and data going back and forth.

Something nice and safe.

Not like this. Cut off from any information. Where the only tech was *none*.

As Kane looked ahead, he realized how good, how helpful it could be to get live sat feeds of everything happening around them, heat signatures showing all enemy combatants, clear satellite shots of any armor moving to box them in. But Command wanted this to end here, and Kane was sure that a surrender was not in the cards. There would be too many questions that way. Too many awkward explanations.

"Keep moving, fast as you can," he said, not that any of the troops needed the urging.

The street—the road to the bridge—had gone quiet. Kane had done enough damage to the enemy at their rear that any force chasing them would need some time to regroup. If they could punch out of the front, they might make it out of the town.

And then? Best not to think about that.

And as if in answer to that thought, he watched two mini-Karelia tanks pivot into place, gun turrets turning, ready to blow his entire group away.

Kane saw his lead marines slow as they spotted the tanks moving into position to box them in. Exactly the wrong move.

His marines had about two, maybe three hundred meters before they reached the tanks. Only seconds before the tanks would be perfectly positioned. Kane, in the lead, looked to the people to his left and right. "We're going to run—and take those out. Now!"

As soon as he broke into that run, his legs aching from everything they had done so far, he could see that it was probably hopeless. They'd be sitting ducks. But then his AAVs behind him opened fire. Kane was close enough to hear the steady plink of the shells hitting the reinforced metal of the tanks ahead, peppering the armored compound that was nearly impenetrable.

And Kane noticed something interesting: the steady shelling seemed to slow the tanks' moves. Could be they had a young crew, borrowed from Russia. The sound, the firing was throwing them off. Then the AAVs each launched RPGs, expertly targeting the tractor base of the tanks. Just as Kane had rehearsed them.

Practice makes perfect.

The shells landed squarely in front of the tracks, near the small triangle that exposed a weak area of the small tank's fronts. Two perfect shots—but were they enough?

Then one of the tanks fired, sending multiple shells flying down the street. They arced over Kane, one mere inches above his helmet.

He spun to see one cannonading shell smash into a group of soldiers hugging the wall in front of the vehicles. The shell exploded, and smoky, reddish mist filed the air.

Shit . . .

Then another hit one of the AAVs and stopped it. Kane waited a moment for anyone to come out. No movement.

Still, the exchange had bought them some time. They had a *shot*. He pointed his machine gun straight ahead, tight in his right hand, while his left ripped off a thermite grenade.

He thought of barking another command at the soldiers with him. But he could see there was no need to do that. This was it—either they'd be able to punch out of the corridor made by this street—or every single marine with Kane would die.

Kane's calves and thighs burned from the full-out run. The single AAV kept tight on their heels, urging them on.

One enemy tank cautiously edged down the street, while the other now appeared immobile. But its turret still looked for a target. Kane and his men were only seconds from where they could toss their grenades. A few of the platoon had rocket launchers strapped to their backs—but there was no time to stop, set them up, launch the weapons.

Just a few more meters . . .

And then he saw one of his marines stop and toss one, then another grenade. It acted like an electric trigger—the air suddenly filled with flying grenades. Then the peppering of automatic fire.

The grenades landed in, on, and around both Karelia-class tanks—and despite the strength of the armored compound shielding them, the tanks exploded into smudgy fires. It was enough to lure the enemy behind them into the opening.

Let's see what we're really dealing with, Kane thought.

The enemy—hidden in the smoke—made the mistake of entering the open street. *Too bad they didn't know their Custer. They could have waited on either side. We'd have no place to go. But now—we get targets.*

And the full platoon, who only seconds ago had been lobbing grenades, started firing at the smoky figures. While the smoke provided the enemy some cover, Kane's marines could see the shrouded shapes appear and could mow them down.

He even felt a little sorry for the bastards. No one wanted this—no one wanted to end their days in some backwater city's grungy street dying for oil that would do you or your family absolutely no good.

We're all the same, Kane thought. *All just pieces being played.*

The enemy fell, bodies collapsing onto other bodies.

He felt his own soldiers pick up their speed, now feeling that they had a way out, that—miraculously—they were going to get out of this thing.

The lone AAV fired another round of rocket shells, pinpointing an area behind the smoke cloud. As good a place as any to hit.

And then—Kane could swear that he didn't see—or hear—any firing from the front.

The platoon reached the dead enemy soldiers, the smoking tanks, and still kept moving quickly. The road led to the main bridge out, and then a narrow highway to the border. Even the newly emboldened Terekstan would be wary of crossing the border. People liked their wars small and contained these days. They passed into an open area; another perfect spot for an ambush. But whatever force had reached the other end of the street had been destroyed. The way ran clear to the bridge, and safety for his company and for the rescued marines.

And for himself—the officer who had carried out this mission against orders?

Well, that would be a different story.

11

FOR A FEW MOMENTS, NOBODY IN THE LARGE CON-
ference room said anything. They just stared mutely
at the screen. Perhaps Hayden had seen this before.
And certainly Kelliher had looked at the image often
enough.

But Ian Kelliher thought it was worth the price of
admission to see the looks on Swann's and Campbell's faces. Jack Campbell was one tough son of a
bitch—but this gave him pause.

Without waiting for anyone to react, Kelliher
touched the tabletop controls. The image began a
slow 360-degree turn, so everyone could look at it
very carefully as it turned.

"Jee-sus . . ." Campbell said.

"Indeed," Kelliher replied. "Quite something,
General, no?"

Hayden nodded.

Kelliher looked back at the thing on the screen. One of the more recent experimental results.

"I believe," Kelliher said, "that this experiment involved increasing the distance of the teleported subject, am I correct?"

"I imagine so. I only get—"

"Right. 'Need to know' basis, and all that bull-shit."

Kelliher realized that he had spat out the last word—he needed to keep his cool here. Hayden—despite his well-honed instincts to hide any facts that might prove troublesome or disturbing to the bureaucratic cosmos—was, in fact, a good honcho to be running this operation.

Like Kelliher, Hayden knew how to inspire fear. Like Kelliher, he believed in the importance of this mission. They had had quiet chats back at the Palo Alto labs, discussing the future of Mars.

Not Earth's future, to be sure. That shithole prob-ably didn't have one. If the people of Earth were to have any hope, Mars would be the key to it. And Hayden could be ruthless. So what was a little lying and duplicity among friends?

"You have seen this before, right, General?"

A pause. Not so long as to be insubordinate, but enough to show that Hayden was weighing the mer-its of his answer . . .

"Yes." Then: "Briefly. Yes, I have."

Kelliher now stepped back as the 3-D image finished its rotation.

"I believe the subject was a primate, correct?"

"A capuchin monkey," Hayden said. "Betruger likes them for their size, their intelligence—a good match, he claimed."

"A good match . . . to humans, that is?"

"Yes."

Now it was Kelleher's turn to pause. A smile in the pale blue light. "Doesn't look very human now, does it? Or much like a monkey, for that matter."

The image had returned to its starting position. Kelliher noted that there was *some* fur on the thing— odd, scruffy patches. And it did have handlike paws. But those "hands" now ended in talonlike claws. A long tail curled out from the creature's rear end, but that was no monkey tail. It looked barbed, with spikes coming out of it. Might work for some deep-ocean giant arachnid.

But on a goddamn monkey? It was the head that was truly the most disturbing. It seemed to have ballooned into an oblong shape. The two eyes had merged into one large, gooey sphere, a dark soulless pupil sitting in some murky greenish-white mucus—a pit of emptiness.

But that was the least of it. The mouth of the "subject" had stretched into a wide, constant grimace. More teeth than any creature could need or ever use. Long fangs, giant chomping molars, set in a mouth that completely dwarfed the head and the rest of the thing.

It looked designed—if that was the right word— for only one thing.

"I never got a report on this, now did I?"

"No, sir. Betruger has asked that all the bad transmissions—"

A full laugh now. "A *bad* transmission? Is that what he calls them?"

"Yes."

"No report. But I assume something happened when this . . . thing arrived in the lab?"

Hayden looked at Swann and Campbell. "Yes. Things happened."

"See—I don't know all about that, General. So before we leave, before I tell you how things will go from here on, for this next crucial year . . . why don't you tell me. Now."

Hayden cleared his throat. Then, as if to reassert some of his status as commander of Mars City, the person actually running this place, Hayden stood up and walked to the image.

"It arrived in the lab . . . alive . . ."

Walker stood up in the main cafeteria, his plate of food mostly uneaten. He looked around the nearly empty room to see who might be looking at him.

Wondering what he was thinking, planning . . .

Because this was something he hadn't talked about with anyone . . . *anyone*. After all, he was told not to talk about what he might see in the lab. The threats were quite clear. A few loose words and he might be in big trouble.

But then Walker had seen something that he wasn't supposed to. He had been standing guard near the north portal. And one of the scientists fell to the ground. Someone yelled for help. Then, quite clearly, the sound and the smell of someone throwing up—

Now Walker reached the trash containers. He scraped his still-full plate into the blue container and placed the tray, the silverware, the smeary plate on the giant plastic yellow tray.

And in the lab on that day, he had moved from his position. He wasn't supposed to do that. Not supposed to move at all from where he was standing.

Not without an order—

But the yelling, the scientist falling, those hacking sounds—

He had hurried toward the center of the lab. A tight circle of scientists were standing around some kind of small glass chamber. Walker's eyes had gone to the guy on the floor. Someone in a white coat saying people should stand back. Another white coat to the side, the guy throwing his guts up—

But then he saw that everyone wasn't looking at either of those two men—

No, the scientists were looking at what was inside the glass chamber—

And in that moment, Walker told himself. This is

wrong. I've read enough stories, seen enough vids to know—

Inside the chamber . . . something alive.

Walker had frozen in his tracks looking at it, the way it kept splashing against the thick clear glass, trying to smash its way out. Or maybe, with the clatter of its clawlike appendages smacking the glass, trying to *claw* its way out.

It was unlike anything he had ever seen. Except in those vids, in those weird stories he read back on the base on Earth.

His first instinct had been to back up. Which is when he noticed that the thing seemed to have turned, to follow Walker's movements. Walker had felt its eyes locked on him, studying him as the claws banged even louder against the glass.

The circle of scientists had also now backed away, but they had looked at Walker, seeing that the thing in the glass case had its eyes on him.

Finally Dr. Betruger's voice had cut through the air. "Everyone, back to work. Get the hell back now."

The head scientist had turned to Walker. The marine had imagined that his eyes must have looked puffy, bulging out of his head. *So goddamn scared . . .*

"You. You . . . listen to me."

Walked pushed open the cafeteria doors. No one was looking at him now. No one could guess his plan. What he was going to do.

Walker had finally looked at Betruger.

"You have seen nothing here, you understand?"

Walker had nodded.

"This is all *top* security. Completely protected by National Security. If you so much"—Betruger had clenched his fists—"as say a goddamn single word about this, then you will spend the rest of your life out there, walking patrol in the goddamn frozen Martian night. You want that?"

Walker had cleared his throat.

"N-no sir. I—"

"Good. Then forget all this. Back to your post."

Walker had walked slowly, taking so much care with every step, and with every step wondering, *Is the thing still looking at me?*

The clattering of the claws had begun to fade. Voices had begun talking again. The sound of something heavy being wheeled away—the glass tank perhaps.

He had finally turned when he was well away, back at his post. The tank had been moved to the rear of the expansive lab.

And that's when Walker had started thinking about his plan.

The door to the cafeteria closed behind him. The hallway was full of people. His hand slid down to his sidearm. He made sure the gun's safety was off. Then he started walking toward Mars City reception.

He'd have to wait. Time his move. It would be tricky. Nobody else knew it yet, but Private James Walker was about to get the hell out of this place.

•   •   •

"So you know guys up here?"

Maria wanted to tell Rodriguez to just give it up. She wasn't on Mars to socialize, and even if she was, it was highly doubtful he'd be the first one she'd hit on.

She looked at the whole Martian experience as a way of escaping all that. For a year. Maybe more. The relationship thing had never been her forte, and this place seemed as good as any for getting away from it.

She glanced at Rodriguez. Not a bad-looking kid, anyway. Being the newbie here, she didn't want to completely blow him off.

"Know? You mean, do I have any friends here?"

"Yeah. I guess."

"No. I came here to get away from whatever friends I had." She fixed the other grunt with her eyes, hoping her next words found their mark. "And I'm not in the market for any new ones."

Rodriguez nodded. "Gotcha. Good place for that. Long shifts. Work you like crazy up here. But good for your bank account. When I get back to Earth, I'm gonna be able to party big-time."

"Good for you," she said, turning away.

She looked at the conference room. Still sealed up tight.

Then she concentrated on her surroundings, looking up and down the corridor. This place could be any subterranean industrial headquarters anywhere on Earth. The lighting, the hallway. Certainly nothing "Martian" about it.

Kelliher had turned off the screen. He heard Swann take a breath.

"Yeah, I know—strong stuff. And whatever that thing was, whatever happened to it due to Betruger's experiments, stands in the way of the promise of teleportation."

"Ian, Dr. Betruger knows that, he—"

"Yeah, yeah, I bet he does. And I bet he has his theories as well. But from my source inside, that's all he has. Some vague ideas about molecular distortions, genetic recombination. All sounds pretty impressive, except it means he doesn't have a clue."

"There are liabilities here, sir."

Kelliher rolled his eyes at Swann's words. "God, don't you think I know that? Of *course*, there are liabilities. I didn't build this entire city for Betruger to cook up genetic mutations, if that's what the hell they are. But he's not an idiot. He knows what this is all about. He'll want to solve the problem."

Here Kelliher looked at Swann and Campbell. He could see from their expressions that his counselor and head of security were suddenly worried that he might tell Hayden something that—as of now—no one on Mars knew. *Do they think I'm that stupid?* "Betruger wants what I want. But his work, this place, needs to be monitored, General. Closely monitored."

"And I am, Ian, I—"

"Of course. But remember I have someone in the lab who will continue sending me updates directly. And these two—"

He nodded to Swann and Campbell.

"—will be, as I said, coming up here regularly. I expect they will get your full cooperation. In addition to the results from Delta, I want updates on the construction progress in general, where things are ahead of schedule, where things are behind. And Site 3? That holds a great personal interest . . . for obvious reasons."

"I'll see that you get all that."

"And see too that Swann and Campbell get it whenever they are here. Free rein. Complete access. Then maybe I can stay on Earth running things . . ."

For as long as I plan on being on Earth.

"I understand," Hayden said tightly. Not a man used to taking orders, Kelliher knew. And he imagined some people would get their ass kicked as soon as he left, just to balance the forces of the universe.

"Great. Then we are—for now—done here. Onward with Mars City. To the future."

The men stood up. Kelliher hit a button and the windows of the conference room became clear, the bustling activity in the admin area suddenly visible, temporarily banishing the horrors they had all just witnessed.

12

AS IF SOMEONE SUDDENLY THREW A SWITCH, THE barrage that had been steadily streaking from Terekstan just ended. Kane thought that the pursuit had been half-hearted anyway. Once they had crossed the bridge, the possibility of a nasty little trap had disappeared. And no air support ever arrived for them . . .

That was the interesting part. Would have been a quick way to take them out—a few heavily armored Russian fighters could have made short work of Kane and his escaping company. So somehow, and from somewhere, an order had gone out. No air support, no firing missiles and plasma rockets at the escaping marines.

Not part of the deal, Kane imagined. The Russians get Terekstan and their oil. And once Kane and his troops were out of the bear trap, they were free to go, across the border and to safety.

Kane could see hills ahead, shadowy on this over-cast night, no glow of moonlight to show what might lay behind. He sat on top of the surviving AAV and turned back to Gonzales. "Anything yet?"

"No, Lieutenant, still all dead, and—wait a sec-ond . . . Yes, we got it now. Sat links logging in, and now, yes, we got a full comm signal. They lifted it, Lieutenant. They lifted the blackout."

Just as Kane thought they would. He had dis-obeyed orders but was now in safe territory, a U.S. ally. *Now they have to talk to us.*

Kane decided to initiate the conversation. He hit the comm button on his PDA. It flashed red, then green. A small screen appeared as it scanned for a signal, and bingo, he was once again linked into the massive communications network of the U.S. De-partment of Defense.

"Lieutenant John Kane, commander of Mustang Company, reporting in."

Nothing for a second. Then a voice, just a radio operator, but tentative, careful. "Lieutenant Kane, we have your position. Proceed in your current vec-tor for 3 point 2 klicks. Then you will come to full stop there, Lieutenant—and wait."

Funny. We break into a town, save another marine company, lose a lot of good men, some maybe because they pulled the plug on all our data feeds. Now they'll talk. Now they'll fucking communicate.

"Copy that."

He knew the AAV driver already had a map and course dumped into her onboard drives. They could actually sit back and let the New Pentagon steer them to the location. And just wait there? For what?

Kane shook his head. He wished Chadbourne was here. Be good to have him to talk to. The rest of the company—well, he didn't have any personal relationship with them. He was the lieutenant—merely there to give the orders. No friendships blossoming here.

So he was left alone with his thoughts about what was ahead now . . . just 2 point 6 klicks ahead . . . 2 point 5.

But he could well imagine.

Kane jumped off the AAV and stood on a flat area, a desolate plain filled with scraggly trees and dotted with clumps of bushes.

A bad thought occurred to him: *We're sitting ducks here.* If something was going to happen, one couldn't ask for a better ambush site. But no—there couldn't be any ambush planned. Not if they were back on SatLink. The whole world could watch whatever went down here. Unlike the sacrifice in the city that the honchos at the New Pentagon had wanted.

"Lieutenant, order your troops to stand down."

Kane nodded. No point having them attempting to look like a fighting army. And most of them didn't have a clue that what they had done wasn't about to be viewed as heroic or patriotic. That it was, in fact, a violation of a direct order. They'd learn soon enough.

"Lieutenant Kane, we will be rendezvousing with you in t-minus-60 seconds."

"Roger that."

And yes, now he heard the engines. Heavy-duty battle choppers, coming from the southeast. A lot of them, from the growing noise.

The marines, who had been sitting on the ground, quickly stood up. *Easy*, Kane thought. *Just some of our own guys coming to take us home. Most of us, anyway.*

Then the air above this low depression became ringed by the giant choppers, their tungsten lamps making it daylight. The marines on the ground covered their eyes.

Come on, Kane thought. *Back the hell off. Turn off the damn light show. These poor bastards have just fought their way out of hell.*

Kane watched as the massive choppers fired burners that turned them immediately vertical and then, like giant solemn totems, they lowered themselves to the ground.

One of his marines came up to Kane. "Lieutenant, should we do anything?"

"Yeah," Kane said. "Watch. Should be an interesting show."

The choppers came to rest girding the company. Kane hadn't done a lot of time in them, but he knew that each interior could pivot on its own gimbal system so that whatever force was inside could be quickly disgorged. Each chopper could hold nearly a company, plus a few attack vehicles, all ready to erupt from the chopper's belly in a heartbeat.

Which was exactly what happened.

With perfect timing, on someone's command, the choppers' doors flew open and marines streamed out. Fresh, unmarred from any battle. A few small armored vehicles rolled out of a pair of the choppers.

But mostly it was just marines. They fell into formation.

Kane heard a voice in his ear. "Lieutenant Kane, this is Captain Patel. Order your men to fall in and await orders from my lieutenants."

Lieutenants? Guess I'm about to be relieved.

"Yes, sir."

"Lieutenant, you will deliver your sidearms to Lieutenant Carp when he reaches your position. You will then be placed under military arrest."

Kane could already see the newly arrived troops encircling his marines, while lieutenants barked orders. *Careful here*, Kane thought. His company and the one he rescued had been through a lot. Best not to overdo the gung-ho. He watched one group of marines—some of those who had been trapped inside the city—being marched toward one of the choppers.

"Lieutenant?" Kane turned to face another marine lieutenant who was looking at him, flanked by three soldiers, guns at the ready.

Kane glanced from the lieutenant to the accompanying soldiers, weapons ready.

"What do you think I'm going to do? Run? Fight?"

"Sorry, Lieutenant, but you must turn over your sidearm to me now." Kane nodded. Not unexpected.

Military arrest. Then some months down the road, court-martial, then what? A cell in some bugfuck part of the U.S., maybe in the dust bowl? With crops a thing of the past, they needed the business.

"I understand," Kane said. He smiled at the lieutenant, whose eyes seemed wide, worried. *What the hell did they tell him about me? Watch out, he might snap, might go for his weapon. Maybe they'd like that.*

Kane gestured at the shoulder strap for his machine gun and at the holder for his pistol. "You mind?"

The lieutenant shook his head. "Best you let my men remove the weapon."

"Right. Sounds good to me too."

The young lieutenant nodded, and the three soldiers came over to Kane, their eyes on his as they removed first his machine gun, then his pistols, then began unclipping his thermite grenades from his vest. Until all his weapons were gone.

I'm nice and safe now, Kane thought. *How much time will I get?* Refusing a direct order in time of war. With war constant now, the military was on a permanent war footing. Couldn't be sure, but had to be a long fucking time.

"Lieutenant Kane, pursuant to the Articles of War and the 2126 Military Council Ruling, you will be put under military arrest and remanded back to the United States for court-martial."

"The charge?" Kane said. He knew damn well what the charge was. But he wanted to hear this spiffy lieutenant say the word.

"Direct disobedience of an order while in combat."

Kane smiled. He had disobeyed the order and saved twenty, thirty good marines.

"Yup, that's what it was, Lieutenant. I'm ready to go when you are."

But his captor wasn't done. "One more thing—" The lieutenant nodded to one of the marines with him, and the man grabbed Kane's wrist.

He pulled Kane's arms behind his back, while another guard placed cuffs on him. A beep signaled that the digital lock on the cuffs was closed. Only one thing could get Kane out of those cuffs—a code.

He noticed some of his own company looking back at the brightly lit scene. *See, we're about to screw one of our own. Just for you . . .*

Kane thought that now the show might be over. But the lieutenant walked close and ripped the silver bars from his shoulder.

"You won't be needing these anymore, Kane."

Then the guards forcibly turned Kane around and steered him in the direction of a waiting chopper. An empty one, it appeared. Under orders, he imagined, to take the war criminal directly back to the States . . . and to face his fate.

13

THE GENERAL CAME OUT OF THE CONFERENCE room first, nodding to Moraetes. Their orders, she knew, were to accompany the party to Reception and on to the main embarkation area.

God, then maybe she could ditch Rodriguez and his nonstop chatter for a bit. If Mars was a place for her to advance, she was pretty sure that it was not by assignments like this, with an idiot like him.

She fell behind the four men making their way to the shuttle that would bring them back to the orbiting carrier and their ride home.

The men moved slowly, so Maria kept her steps small. *And what are we doing here*? she wondered. *Guarding them?* An escort. Seemed kind of odd, when they could just walk from Admin over to the shuttle. What could happen?

She saw one of the men turn and look at her. He had the face and build of someone who had done some military time, and clearly had risen through the ranks.

He stared at Maria. Giving her the once-over. Most men would expect a woman, even a space marine, to turn away.

But this guy (she caught a bit of his name tag on his UAC uniform: *Camp*—) yeah, this guy didn't know Maria's history, her background. Why she was here and why maybe even Mars wasn't far enough to get away. And her bold stare right back at him made him turn away.

Private James Walker had walked around one corner, then turned left, retracing his steps. He kept his eyes straight ahead, walking slowly and steadily. So that if anyone saw him, they wouldn't think *anything*.

His right hand brushed his holstered pistol as he walked. Just the casual back and forth motion of an arm as you walked. Nothing odd about that. Nothing anyone might notice. Save for the fact that the holster was unbuckled. Nobody would see that.

And now Walker moved into Reception. He didn't look at the two people at the desk, acting as if Mars City was some kind of tourist destination. Two armed guards stood to either side of the desk. Any one of them could ask what he was doing. *Hey, where you going, Private? Have clearance for this area?*

Because that was the interesting thing. You needed clearance to move from one area to another in Mars City. And there were dozens of clearance levels.

As soon as Walker entered the reception area, he was completely out of his clearance area. A few things would now happen very rapidly.

The sensors throughout Mars City would search for a chip embedded somewhere inside his body and recheck his clearance. The system would then begin the first stage of a security process—*Private James Walker is not in an area where he has clearance.* Then the system would check all outstanding orders entered by any outstanding superior on Mars—civilian or military—who may have ordered Walker to go somewhere, do something in a place he had no business in.

That would turn up negative.

At that point—and Walker was not too sure about this part—an alarm of some kind would be issued. Not an emergency lockdown, because casual orders were given all the time, updated via PDAs that fed into whatever computer net handled the commands.

So before a full alarm could be issued, a quick request would go out first to Walker, enquiring what he was doing. Who ordered him to come to this place?

Simultaneously, another request would go out to anyone who had supervisory contact with Walker. Had an order been given and not entered?

All this—happening now, so fast. No matter.

Walker had waited in the cafeteria, watching. Any alarm would arrive too late.

He turned toward the embarkation area. Where the doors—of course—did not open. No security clearance, and every invisible scan looking at him noted that not only could he not pass through the doors, but he shouldn't even be standing near them.

Walker turned to the right, toward a small alcove with a control board monitoring the environmental status of this section of Mars City. He walked up to it, touched his earpiece as if getting a message. He nodded.

No one could really see him here. But if they did, they'd see a marine nodding, listening, perhaps getting orders.

He heard steps. Voices. They were here. His hand went to his gun.

"Just as soon as we get back to Earth, my office will coordinate Swann's and Campbell's schedules with you, General," Kelliher said to Hayden.

"Whenever they want to come—"

"It'll be more formal than that. I want detailed reports from them. Pictures. Interviews. As if I'm here."

Hayden nodded. "I understand."

Kelliher imagined that Hayden couldn't wait until Kelliher and his two men were gone. And then, pity the poor marines who got in his way. Asses would be chewed up and spit out.

"Dr. Betruger—what information should he—"

"Minimal. He'll know that I have my counselor and security people here. And he knows of my interests. But he doesn't need to know . . . just how much I am keeping tabs on him . . . and—"

They had walked past Reception, down the wide corridor leading to one of the embarkation portals, this one used by guests and VIPs primarily.

Something made Kelliher slow down. Instinct. Something that had guided him for many years.

Slow now, but he didn't stop. Until they were at the doors, the scanner reading their clearance, recording thermal scans, making sure they were allowed to enter the massive hangar that led to the shuttle, and home. *Home for now*, Kelliher thought.

Something to the left caught his eye. A control board filled with colored lights, and someone standing there. A marine.

Instinct . . .

Kelliher looked at the twin doors swinging wide open. His personal PDA buzzed in his pocket. A low tone filled the room. An alarm. No screeching high-pitched noise. Alarms went off frequently up here. But this one—a low thumping noise like a heartbeat filled the room with a dull throbbing.

The doors opened. But the soldier was in motion. Kelliher saw quite clearly that the man had his gun out.

For a second Kelliher debated: dash through the open doors, or turn back. A few seconds of indecision. But enough for the soldier, his gun raised high, to be on him, the barrel tucked neatly under Kelliher's chin. And then the voice, a small, hoarse voice, empty of anything.

"Keep moving, Mr. Kelliher. Keep moving to the shuttle."

Maria immediately lowered her rifle, as did Rodriguez.

She also spotted that one of the other men—Campbell—had quickly gotten a gun out. But the marine—not anyone Maria had seen before—also saw their weapons.

"Put them down! Put them the hell down now or he gets it."

Kelliher looked at them all. "Do as he says. *Now.*"

Rodriguez was first to get his gun down. Then Campbell. The guy had his eyes on Maria, which told her a lot.

She slowly started to lower her weapon.

The first thing: she saw fear. This guy was completely scared. Whatever he was afraid of had to be worse than taking the man who owned Mars City hostage.

The second thing: she saw insanity there. Not surprising. You had to be more than crazy to do this. Scared and crazy—not a good combination. But one that—unknown to anyone in this little grouping—she had seen and dealt with before.

By now they had entered Hangar One. Smaller

shuttles sat to the side, while a good-sized shuttle or-
biter was only meters away. It would then taxi out of
one of the large hangar portals and take off for Kelliher's UAC transport ship, now orbiting Mars.

They kept walking.

The man whispered in Kelliher's ear, "You're
going . . . to take me with you, you hear me? On the
shuttle. And once there, I'm going back to Earth with
you."

Kelliher nodded, wondering: Had this nutcase
thought through *any* of this? Did he really think he
could get away with it? And what would happen
when he got back to Earth? Ask for a jet waiting,
loaded with unmarked bills?

Or maybe he didn't care about that. Insane people
will do anything.

The shuttle was now only meters away. Guards
and UAC people were all over, but no one would
dare be stupid enough to make a move.

Campbell and Swann followed.

Kelliher saw that the two escorts—the two marines, now weaponless—kept following. That seemed
to catch his captor's attention, now only meters away
from the shuttle gantry.

"You—you two. Stop right there! What the hell
you doing?"

Maria kept her eyes on the man, his finger tight
around the trigger. It wouldn't take much for that

nervous finger to send the UAC head honcho's brains onto the floor.

But as she looked at the crazy man—the soldier who was quite clearly terrified—she knew that he didn't want that. No, all he wanted was to get on the shuttle with Kelliher, to get off this planet, to escape. But if he felt he had a chance, a slim possibility of achieving his goal, he would hold that finger tight and hope to hell he didn't have to pull it.

Kelliher muttered to the two men with him. "Don't you move." Then to his captor: "It's all going to be fine, son, just fine—"

Good, she thought. *Kelliher's trying to reassure him. All will be okay. Everything will work out just the way he hoped it would. Just let him think that . . .*

One step. Then another. Her movements tiny. But she saw Kelliher's eyes go to her in horror. *No . . . ,* those eyes screamed. *Don't do a thing.*

And Maria guessed if it was her brains up for grabs, she might want things to freeze. But events like this only got worse. The guy could panic. Lots of people could get hurt.

Now, when it was unexpected, it was time to make a move.

Another step. Her gun not raised, but not thrown to the floor as Rodriguez's was. She pulled her right hand back, then she turned a bit as if Kelliher's look had actually had some impact, as if she was going to turn back those few steps and walk back to Rodriguez.

Her body twisted to the right, arm pulled back, palms open, rising up now until it was at shoulder height. And then she uncoiled her twisting body, let her open palm—now curling, balling—fly.

If she hit her mark, her hand would catch the soldier on the side of his head. His head would then snap back, and the gun would jerk away from under Kelliher's chin. If she was wrong . . .

Her fist flew into the side of the soldier's skull. He staggered back, not seeing it come at all. Then the gun moved—just as Maria had known it must.

His finger probably tightened even as the barrel began to slip.

There wasn't time for a second punch from her, not before the barrel began its flight and the man's finger fully tightened. The explosion of the sidearm suddenly filled the cave of the hangar. Now Maria launched her second blow while trying to see just how badly things had gone.

Kelliher was kneeling on the floor. The hostage-taker still had his gun. Not good at all.

The other marines who had been standing nearby started to scramble for their weapons, wasting precious seconds. She kept coming at the guy. A strong shot to his midsection and he lost the ability to breathe. She grabbed his hand, the one holding the gun, tightening on the wrist, which she twisted as if unscrewing a massive cap. The gun fell to the floor.

She released the wrist and then sent the same hand, now once again a traditional fist, into the soft side of the soldier's cheek. A jarring hit that could knock him out, or at the very least send him to the floor in agony.

He went flying back. The other marines were all over him, almost comical in their overkill. Maria turned.

Kelliher was bleeding. She saw him look at his wound and then at her, as a medical team arrived.

General Hayden walked over to Maria. "You'd best report to your quarters, Private. I will call you when I am ready to speak with you."

Maria nodded, then, remembering: "Yes, sir."

She stepped back. The head of the UAC was bleeding on the hangar floor. Then it dawned on her: she had just played roulette with the life of one of the most powerful men on Earth.

After saluting, she started walking back to her quarters.

14

MARS CITY

HOURS LATER, PRIVATE MARIA MORAETES STOOD outside General Hayden's office. Finally, she heard a barely audible signal coming from the headset of Hayden's adjutant.

"Yes, sir. I'll send her right in." The adjutant looked up. "The general will see you now."

Maria nodded. The door slid open, and she walked into the office.

She took in the details. The room, filled with rich wood, looked like a military officer's room from another century. A massive wooden desk with claw feet dominated much of the room.

General Hayden looked down at the desk, then, without giving Maria a glance, he went to his screen. After what seemed an eternity, he looked up at her.

"I was going to ask you, Private Moraetes, whatever possessed you to do . . . what you did. But you know what? I'm not really interested."

"Sir, I saw Mr. Kelliher in danger and I thought—"

"Oh, *thinking*, are we? Didn't know that privates were expected to actually think. Here's the news flash—same here as down on Earth. No thinking required. Just follow orders."

"The situation . . . was complicated, sir. And I—"

"Yeah, complicated. So you take action that could have killed Ian Kelliher. As it was, he took a shot. Delayed his return home. Could have killed him."

Maria hesitated a moment She imagined that saying nothing might be the best course. Screw it.

"He could have been *killed*, sir."

"Or we could have defused the situation later. Crazy bastard trying to get off Mars. He could have been talked down, Private. There was no call for your risky move, your potentially deadly actions."

Hayden fixed her with his eyes as if daring her to again attempt an explanation. She wanted to ask where the soldier came from. Did the general know what made him act? But she said nothing.

Then the general pointed at the screen. "But I see here in your personnel record what may have prompted you to do that. God, the flotsam and jetsam we get sent up here. Mars City, home to an amazing array of not-quite marines. Like you. But I see you got a bit of a story here."

Maria knew what he was looking at. Buried in her personnel file. And yes, maybe what he saw did have something to do with the action she took.

"I never hid my past, General. I—"

His hand shot up.

"No. And we all know it now. Know it and—"he tapped his skull—"we can remember. You're one lucky marine, Moraetes. Lucky that Kelliher is alive. Lucky that he doesn't want your ass for the risk you took."

Again Maria thought: *I saved him. Ian Kelleher's brains could be spread all over the hangar floor. I saved him.* But it was useless to say anything.

"We're done here, Private. And I do hope that for as long as I am on Mars, and you are, that our paths don't ever cross again. Dismissed."

Maria saluted sharply. Turning on her heels, she walked out of the office, the sliding door whooshing open, then quickly shutting behind her.

She had hoped that the military would be different. That what happened below, down on Earth, might not happen here. That a new world might mean things might just be less about bullshit, less about lies and covering your ass.

And now Maria knew that she was wrong. It would be a long two years ahead for her on Mars. . . .

Dr. Kellyn McDonald walked to one of the side corridors of Delta. This particular corridor, leading to a series of storage areas, required the highest possible security clearance.

He had heard about the attack that nearly cost Ian Kelliher his life. And MacDonald thought he might have seen the soldier who had snapped, only recently posted to Delta, along with other new space marines. Only this guy happened to see something that he really shouldn't have.

And it scared him enough that his terrified mind cooked up a plan to escape. To get the hell off Mars. Maybe not such a crazy idea, MacDonald thought. Maybe the crazy ones were the people staying here.

Meters away from the lab doors, a scanner picked up the ID on his lab coat, then confirmed his ID via a thermal scan while he walked slowly down the corridor. The electronic doors opened, carefully sensing that only the person with the proper security walked through. No own would pay much attention to MacDonald coming down here. He could be doing a dozen things—looking for equipment, checking some supplies. There were a dozen storerooms here.

But his clearance allowed him everywhere. He wanted access only to the storeroom at the far end. Here, he had to manually enter a code—just one more layer of protection.

He entered a small storage area that faced a massive freezer that filled the room. Not for food. Not for medical equipment. Over one thousand square feet of frozen storage space. And already getting full.

Cameras all around the room followed his movements. But there would be no alert, no reason for anyone to be concerned. MacDonald had every right to come in here.

He opened the freezer door. The icy air hit him, chilling him, and gooseflesh rose.

He saw the rows of shelves, the upper tiers empty, those at the bottom full. Row after row of sealed plastic bags. Body bags—only whatever bodies filled these bags came in all different sizes and shapes.

MacDonald slid his PDA from his side. He held it close to his lips. "Record," he said.

Then he clipped the compact data device to a lapel of his coat. He walked over to one bag and unzipped it. Then another. Another. Until he had a half dozen or more bags unzipped. Even with the cold, there was the smell. He fought against the gag reflex.

Five below in here, and still the overwhelming smell . . .

And with the bags open, he started back, peeling away the plastic openings, exposing what lay beneath. Without taking the bodies completely out, it would be hard to really see them. Hard to really make out what you were looking at. But you could see the arms on one corpse, the spidery arms sprouting from a nearly human torso, human, that is, if you didn't look at the scrambled eggs of eyes, ears, and teeth that topped them.

Each one different. Each monstrosity some brand-new combination of horrors.

He hurried, walking down the row. Just wanting to capture a half-dozen images or so. Send them back to Earth. Keep Kelliher fully informed. He had already seen a lot, but he hadn't seen these yet . . .

The latest test results. *Here's what they looked like.*

He got to the last bag. On this one, the primate-like hands ended in clawlike fingers ringed with teeth. As he stood by that one, one of those arms . . . moved. Sliding down, away from the body, pointing down. MacDonald jumped back.

Just happened to slide out of the bag a bit. But now . . . now he'd have to grab the arm and tuck it back in. He gingerly grabbed the dangling arm just above the wrist, taking care not to let his own fingers touch the claw-fingers. Slowly, carefully, McDonald stuffed it back in the bag. Then he pulled the zipper tight.

"End," he whispered to his PDA. Then: "Send encoded. Ian Kelliher."

And even deep within this frozen meat-locker of horrors, the file of images was being encrypted, relayed to the new comm center, and beamed to Earth in a totally secure packet that only Kelliher could unpack once he was back on the planet.

MacDonald turned and walked out of the freezer.

(Not, though, without a look over his shoulder. All those things so dead—but still he had to *look*.)

He shut the freezer. Still rows of shelves to fill. Rows awaiting the next results, the next outcome of Betruger's experiments on Mars. It was, after all, why this was being done here. Nobody to see, nobody to ask questions. Kelliher had planned that.

And as MacDonald reentered the corridor leading back to the main area of Delta, he thought, *We're just getting started here.*

2145

TWO

15

Mars City PDA
Dr. Kellyn McDonald
Personal Folder, Security Enabled.
Checked and Opened_2_05_2145 16:08:19

Dr. Betruger confirmed what the core scientific team has long suspected. Namely, he will proceed post haste with more experiments using "volunteers." Though these steps must be approved on some level by the UAC, and hence Ian Kelliher, I will continue to send full documentation and a warning.

This new series of experiments is alarming for a number of reasons. First, the so-called test results from this past year's work remain largely unexplained. There have been theories, such as spontaneous genetic mutation and even one concept dubbed "telemetric gene modification." But still, no one knows what happened.

And everyone saw what happened to the first human subject. We all watched as a human subject, a marine, stepped into the large chamber, prepared to travel through space, to a distance 20 meters away. Betruger argued that the series of successful teleports of inanimate objects, as well as a few somewhat successful animal "ports," all argued for a human test.

But even those few successful animal subjects later developed difficulties and behavioral changes that remain unexplained. I plan on continuing to record the results of all these new experiments here. I will also inform Kelliher of each step—though I fear he knows, and approves—and my role as his eyes and ears is a false one.

If these steps do not alarm him—if this work doesn't horrify him—then nothing will.

My wife pleads for me to return, this time for good. She may be right. But I have to wonder: would I even be allowed to leave?

Folder Closed and Locked_2_05_2145 16:08:19

16

THE GUARD UNDID THE CUFFS HOLDING JOHN Kane's wrists together. Kane squinted as bright shafts of manufactured sunlight streamed down the hallway from massive phony windows.

His cell had only one small square backlit by a single bright bulb. But this part of the New Pentagon looked as though it was bathed in tropical sunlight, instead of buried deep below the rocky ground.

After the destruction of the old Pentagon in 2078, this new building was designed, as everyone knew, with some key advantages. First, it was located somewhere in Wyoming. The government confirmed that it had been built near Laramie, although layers of secrecy apparently covered all the workers and contractors who built it.

But no matter if any enemy located it. The New

Pentagon was buried so deep, under so much mountainous rock, that it would be impervious to any attack. Or so the Departments of Homeland Security and Defense believed.

When the cuffs were off, a marine captain walked up to Kane. "My name is Captain Ferrita. I will be representing you in the proceedings."

"Yes, Captain."

Kane had been stripped of all rank. He knew he was no longer a lieutenant, but was he even a private? Was he still even in the marines?

He also now knew the punishment for what he had done. When the country was on a permanent war footing, any disobedience of any order in combat could be penalized by death. It was what Kane expected. And after months sitting in the cell below, he might even be ready for that. Otherwise—in this place—madness loomed.

"You are to say nothing unless directly addressed. Charges will be read. The court-martial counsel will consult with the trial board. They may wish to speak with me if there is a possibility of a lesser charge."

"Lesser charge?"

"Yes. A charge less than treason. A situation where you might not face execution."

"How . . . hopeful?"

"Look, Kane. I don't know whether you want to live or not. In fact, to be honest, I don't even care. You are quite clearly guilty. But on the off chance—"

The captain looked Kane in the eyes, and Kane

could see that though the man was nearly a foot shorter, there was some steel there. This military lawyer had seen some things. He didn't blink easily . . .

"—that you *do* want to live, do exactly what I say. Understand?"

"Perfectly."

"Then let's go in."

They took their seats at a polished metal desk that reflected the bright overhead lights. Kane could see the brass sitting in the front, on a raised dais. Two men, one woman, all marines. Turning right, Kane could also see the prosecutor, a thin, reedy-looking marine lawyer who looked like he wouldn't know which end of a gun to point.

The woman—her nameplate said Colonel Thompson—spoke first. "Captain Ferrita, has your client been fully briefed on the charges and possible outcomes he faces?"

Ferrita stood up. "Yes, Colonel. And we hope to make a case today that the circumstances that Lieutenant Kane faced—"

A general at the end, General Schine, jumped in. "*Former* Lieutenant Kane, Captain. Your client has, under military law, been stripped of his rank."

"Yes, sir. Sorry. Now if I—"

Kane watched General Schine cover his mic, then lean over to the man in the middle. And there was something familiar about him. Had Kane seen him in some theater or other? General Hadfield, his name-plate said.

Hadfield whispered to first one then another member of the tribunal. Then he spoke. "Captain Ferrita, we appreciate that you want to do what you can for your client. And we also understand that you think you can make a case of extreme mitigating circumstances regarding former Lieutenant Kane's disobedience of a direct order—"

"Well, of course, but—"

But Hadfield didn't really want an answer from Ferrita. Instead, Kane saw the general give a nod to the prosecution desk, and the rail-thin prosecutor walked up to the table in the front.

Hadfield held up a hand. "Hold on a minute, Captain."

Again some more off-the-record words. Kane leaned close to Ferrita. "I think the term for this is railroad." Ferrita looked back at him with a look that said, *Right, and there's nothing the hell we can do about it.*

Ferrita seemed about to add something, and Kane thought: *Is Ferrita in on whatever is going on here too? Is this little stage play all for my benefit and the record?*

The prosecutor nodded and left the tribunal table.

"There is no need at all for us to review the events of last April, 2144. The electronic record is quite complete; the satellite vids show it all. And I am sure, Captain, you have no wish to waste the tribunal's time, especially with our nation facing threats from so many different sectors."

When in doubt, wave the flag and ditch rights. A pretty old story, Kane thought.

"No, sir. But my client still would like to explain—"

"Mr. Kane, we have—in consultation with the prosecution—discussed an arrangement that would both appease military justice in these difficult days and resolve this case quickly. That is, if you and your lawyer agree to the terms."

Ferrita leaned close. "Think you best stand, since he's talking to you."

Kane stood up. Months sitting in a cell had left Kane stiff. But he still knew he was the only one in the room who had faced anything approaching battle conditions for years. He could feel it. And he knew they could.

"Yes, sir. An arrangement?"

The woman, Colonel Thompson, smiled. "A *deal*. That will allow us to close this matter and all get on with more important work. It will have the advantage, quite possibly, of saving your life."

"Not," General Schine, said, "that we all agree it should be saved."

"A deal?" Kane repeated.

"Yes. And for the particulars, you can follow the prosecution attorney, Colonel Sack, to the conference room. When he has your decision, we will reconvene."

The three stood up. The prosecutor stood to one side, looking almost afraid as he waited for Kane.

Kane turned to Ferrita, eyes locked on him. "Did you know about this 'deal'?"

The captain rubbed his chin, then looked away. "I heard some rumblings that—"

"Rumblings?" Kane shook his head. "Okay then . . . counselor. Let's go see what kind of deal the U.S. Marine Corps has cooked up for me."

He turned and walked toward the prosecutor, already hurrying to the conference room.

Colonel Sack, looking nervous, stood at the end of the room and gestured to two chairs. *I'm not going to hurt you*, Kane thought. *Though that would certainly be fun.*

Kane took a chair and sat down, followed by Ferrita.

He turned to his lawyer, "I would have liked some warning . . . you know, a heads-up?"

"I wasn't sure . . . this would happen." Sack cleared his throat. "As you know, Mr. Kane, your offense carries—in the time of war—the potential of the death penalty."

"Yeah—never a good idea to save other marines. I'll try to remember that."

"Um, but that's just it. The Corps recognizes that what you did, you did to save fellow marines."

"Nice of them to see that."

"Easy, Kane," Ferrita said.

"And a trial dragging up testimony over such an

incident, especially with the other geopolitical realities tossed in—"

"Those realities. You gotta hate them . . ."

"Bottom line: the Corps would like to avoid a trial. It has no interest in exacting the full penalty from you. Instead, it has an offer to make."

"We're listening," Ferrita said.

"Here it is. Kane will be restored to active duty effective within the next forty-eight hours. He will be a private . . . in the space marines."

Kane shook his head. "What? The space marines?" Everyone in the real armed services knew that they were having trouble getting people to sign on to this new subset of the marines. "Might as well agree to be a rent-a-cop."

"The space marines," Sack continued, "serve an important role in the expanding intersolar system security and goals of the United States. You will receive pay commensurate with your new rank, and even be eligible for retirement."

"How long a commitment?" Ferrita asked.

The question seemed to make the prosecutor squirm. "Ten years, nonnegotiable."

Space marines, Kane thought. There could only be a few possibilities. Doing transport security, or escorts for planetary runs, maybe a post to the new Europa project, or the biggie—the project everyone knew about, but *didn't* know anything about. Mars.

"Let me guess, I won't be staying on Earth?"

"They want to send you to Mars City. A minimum of two years on Mars. After that, maybe other postings. That, with your loss of rank, is the deal."

Kane looked at Ferrita. "Any negotiating moves to pull here, counselor?"

But the prosecutor responded fast. "Mr. Kane, there are no other arrangements that can be made. You either accept this or face the tribunal, which could—as you have been told—result in a death sentence."

Kane smiled at the man. "Thanks for the clarification." He stood up. "And when would I leave for Mars?"

"Oh, I thought that was clear. As soon as possible. Forty-eight hours, most likely. With the next major transport. Should be enough time to get your affairs on Earth—whatever they are—in order. So—shall I inform the tribunal that terms have been agreed to?"

"My affairs. Yeah, plenty of time to get them . . . in order." Kane laughed, then stuck out his hand to the prosecutor. "You got a deal."

The prosecutor looked warily at the outstretched hand but took it anyway. Then Kane closed. Not so bad that he'd render Sack's hand useless, but enough so he felt a good strong jolt of pain. Then he released it.

Ferrita stood up. "Private, I'll walk you back to your cell block. They'll get your personal property ready." He turned to Sack. "You will get all the necessary approvals into the pipeline?"

A still-wincing Sack took out a PDA and projected a touch screen that floated a few feet in front of him. He hit some points on the floating screen. "There. Done. Just got to make sure you are at the Denver transport dock at least two hours before departure. You will be ferried up to the main UAC transport out of California. And that"—he took a breath—"is it."

Ferrita put a hand on Kane's shoulder. "Let's go— you've some things to do to get ready . . ."

And just like that, Kane was out of his cell, and back in the marines.

Though not really the marines, he knew. No way you could mix up the space marines with the real deal. As much as they tried to paint it as an elite corps, nobody wanted long tours of guard duty some-where *out there*, whether it was one of the space sta-tions, the moon, Mars, or any of the newer outposts being set up by the UAC. Better than a firing squad, though. Not that they would use such a dramatic form of execution in the twenty-second century. An electric charge to the brain precisely applied would more likely have been the method. Rest in peace.

Ferrita handed him an envelope.

"Here's everything you will need. Embarkation instructions, your CO at the station, a guide to life in zero gravity. Normally they would provide some training, but—"

"They just can't wait to get rid of me?"

They had reached the elevator that would take

them from the depths of this subterranean fortress back to the surface.

Captain Ferrita looked right and left. "Look, Kane. This may be a new chance for you."

"You don't sound so sure."

"I mean, it's better than the alternative. But I think—well—there are rumors all around this place. About Mars. About what's going on there."

"They're building a city, right? A home for the future. Experimental labs, some secret things, right?" Kane looked at the captain, trying to figure out how much he really knew.

"Sure, that's what the vids show. That's what the UAC promotes. Some people are already living there, working and living on Mars. The new frontier and all that. But I got to tell you"—another glance left and right, making sure they were alone—"that isn't the whole story."

"And you think it has something to do with my going up?"

Ferrita nodded. "I don't *know* anything. All I know is what I hear, just the rumors. What people have whispered about. The UAC's experiments, some gone wrong. Some people missing. People get scared. Word filters back. It's getting real tense up there, Kane. And I think, maybe . . . that's why you're going up there."

"Let's send the marine traitor from Terekstan to Mars?"

"Something like that. They're beefing up their marine muscle on the planet. The UAC is worried about something. They pay the freight, the marines supply the bodies. Obviously they thought someone like you would be useful on the planet."

"Useful? Interesting word. Useful for what? Against what?"

The elevator door opened—an empty chamber.

"Wish the hell I knew, Kane. But if I was you, I'd be prepared for anything." Ferrita took a breath.

Least he got that off his chest, Kane thought. A vague warning of something waiting on Mars. And in a funny way, it somehow made Kane feel a little bit better about this unwanted posting.

Suddenly, he thought, things indeed sounded . . . interesting.

17

DR. MALCOLM BETRUGER LOOKED AT THE TEAM of scientists standing in a circle around him. Not one of them did he trust.

No, as soon as this work *changed*, as soon as things became truly exciting, revolutionary, and, yes, frightening, he could sense the shift. He knew they must talk among themselves. Whispers, grumbles perhaps. Did Kelliher have a spy among them? He wouldn't be surprised.

So Betruger had started treating them differently.

First, he began compartmentalizing their responsibilities. Now each one of the esteemed team would function—in their area—alone, and report only to him. While he didn't actually forbid any discussion between any members, he certainly made it clear that he didn't like it.

And that was the other thing. *Fear . . .* Was there a better motivator? A year ago Betruger had looked up to these people as true collaborators, but now each could be a conspirator, someone who might betray the project.

At first they didn't seem so terribly upset by the animal experiments when some went wrong. But they almost all protested the idea of using a human.

Betruger reminded then: *We're on Mars. There is a reason these experiments are being done here.*

The first transfer of a human seemed, initially, to go well. That is, until the private stumbled out of the chamber. He tried to speak. His mouth opened.

"Just rattled by the process," Betruger offered.

But when the volunteer opened his mouth, everyone saw that the man couldn't speak because he had no tongue. No teeth either. In fact, his throat seemed to be bubbling up a fountain of blood, shooting it across the lab floor.

The man was dead within minutes.

That was when Betruger had to shock each and every one of them with his speech. "It means *nothing.* And we will achieve nothing unless we experiment, unless we learn what works and what doesn't."

But even Betruger at first had to wonder. *Losing a tongue? Could that really be part of the transfer process?*

An autopsy report, done right in Delta, was sent only to him. While there were mumblings about shock, about the volunteer marine biting and swallowing his own tongue, the autopsy report showed something quite different.

The tongue, in fact the whole inner mouth, the palate, a chunk of the throat lining had been—it appeared—serrated away. Somehow . . . cut out. Now that was intriguing. And wasn't that what true scientists live for?

As for the second subject, he appeared perfectly fine. A true success. Some of the scientists even applauded like it was a stage show!

The man emerged from the second tank with no signs of anything wrong. He stumbled a bit, his eyes looked around the room. The medical team caught him just as he was about to collapse, then they laid him down on the stretcher.

A success.

Human teleportation across a distance of 30 meters! And the man was fine. But then he woke up. And screamed . . .

They were too late getting the gurney straps onto the man. He attacked one of the nurses, his teeth closing on her shoulder, brutally ripping out a chunk of flesh, then he leaped—with what seemed an almost inhuman strength—onto one of the scientists, grabbed his skull, prepared to bite down.

Only the swift butt of a rifle from one of the guards got the man off. They knocked him out with Coticin, the high-speed supernarcotic, taking him down immediately.

And whenever he was allowed to emerge from his

drug-induced sleep, the screaming would begin again, the straps would look as though they would break.

Betruger ordered him to remain sedated. At least until he knew what happened.

And something he didn't tell anyone, not certainly the scientific team, so much more interesting than mere teleportation. Betruger had ideas—theories— but he kept them to himself. After all, there was no one to trust.

Now, he looked at the assembled scientists. "I want you to prepare for the next test."

He watched their faces, the lack of enthusiasm. Such timid rabbits of science. "And yes," Betruger continued, "it will be a new human experiment."

Maria put her tray down at a table filled with grunts. Two of them, Andy Kim and Dick "Deuce" Howard, had made PFC—private first class—simply by marking time here. That was pretty much how it went. Put time in, get advanced, get a bit more money, and count the days until your Mars tour was over.

Then, if you were desperate, sign on again. After all, there wasn't much waiting back on Earth.

Rodriguez, sitting to the right, hadn't been promoted. *But that's because he's an idiot,* Maria guessed. Trying to run scams and deals in a small place like this where everything is watched and recorded.

As for Maria, she knew that somehow the black mark on her record was still there. *I should have let the nutcase kill Kelliher.*

"Maria, Maria . . . how go things in the halls of Alpha Labs?"

Her current assignment—security in the hallways around Alpha Labs—was about as dull as things could get. She hoped to get rotated to one of the exterior sites. Guard duty on Mars itself, not inside this nest of hallways and tunnels—that might have been something interesting.

"Exciting as ever, Rodriguez. And you, still hitting on the chippies at Reception?"

He laughed. "I got a lot of fuckin' patience, Moraetes. You may not see any of the Rodriguez charm, but they will. And just imagine . . ." He leaned close to her. "All those months with no man-action. Can do wonders to a girl's insides."

Deuce leaned across the table. "Yeah, like make someone desperate enough for a taste of Rodriguez?"

The whole table—minus Rodriguez—laughed.

"Funny, Deuce. Like you'd have better luck."

The giant African-American marine took a massive bite of a sandwich he had made. It looked as though he had stuffed everything on offer at the lunch counter between two slices of the soybread. "I don't . . . kiss and tell. And I certainly don't f—"

"Oh spare me, okay?" Maria said.

She felt Andy Kim looking at her. Maria felt that despite their good friendship, Kim was interested in her. Which was too bad. Sweet kid, but Maria sure as hell wasn't going to let herself get involved with anybody here.

"What about you, Moraetes? You think about hooking up with anyone up here?"

Deuce slapped his friend's shoulder. "She hangs with us. And that's plenty, right, Maria?"

She smiled. "Right. You three clowns are more than enough for one woman." She scooped up a forkful of some beef-flavored glop. Who knew what it really was. Who cared.

And she was glad to see that none of her friends—because that was what they were—pushed that question further. They were all space marines, stuck on Mars. That was all that mattered.

A few moments, then Rodriguez cleared his throat. "I hear . . . that they're looking for another volunteer."

And for a moment nobody said anything.

"Whoa, whoa, *whoa!* Hold it up there!"

Graulich had walked to the cave opening to check on the delivery of equipment she had called for hours ago. Now she saw a half-dozen space marines outside their ROV vehicles, hanging around as if this was a day at the beach. *If they weren't wearing helmets, it looks as if they'd be standing around and smoking cigarettes. This is security?* "Who the hell is in charge here?"

The marines all looked around as if no one wanted to step up and claim that role. Finally one of them stepped close to Graulich.

"I am, ma'am."

Ma'am? "It's 'Doctor.' If you're going to address

me as anything, it's *Doctor.*" She felt the other marines looking at each other. She couldn't see them rolling their eyes, but she sure could feel it. "And your name?"

"Sergeant Mathews . . . Doctor."

Graulich stepped closer. Some of the team were checking the crates that had been deposited at the cave entrance. But she imagined they were watching this little scene go down.

"Sergeant Mathews, let me ask you a question."

"Shoot, ma—um, Doctor."

"Do you think . . . do you *imagine* I asked for additional security for this site so that you marines could stand around the entrance as if someone was about to start a barbecue?"

Mathews looked away. She could see how young he was. They took *anyone* for duty up here. Good thing they didn't have to worry about other countries nosing around Mars City and the excavation sites. Or at least, they didn't have to worry about that yet.

"No. I was really waiting to see what you wanted all these marines here for."

"Good. Okay, for starters, Sergeant—get them a good fifty meters away from the entrance. I have more gear coming and I don't need the loaders navigating around them."

Mathews turned. "Okay. *Listen* up, men. Take a position out there"—a confirming look at Graulich—"fifty meters or so."

For a second no one moved. *Guess the marines*

aren't too impressed by Mathews being in charge. But slowly they started trudging away.

He turned back to Graulich.

"Good. Okay, let me explain very clearly what's going to happen, and what you're going to do. You see, in here, we're going to start some days of heavy drilling and explosions. It's what we're supposed to do. And the thing is, no one is supposed to see any of it. Not you, not them. Understand?"

"Yes, I—"

"And I've asked for more security for two reasons, Sergeant. Got your ears on?" He nodded. And she had the thought that maybe she should ease up on him. But no—this was too much fun. *We all need something to ease the tension.* "I don't want, and your general doesn't want, anyone to come near here that isn't supposed to be here. And further, we're not sure what other pockets and holes may open up . . . up here, all around the site as we excavate. So your little band of marines . . . I want them posted all around."

Mathews looked to the cave roof and nodded. "You mean on top, and—what? Surrounding the place?"

"Such a smart marine. If they see anything, any opening that—again—we don't want anyone entering, they let you know and then you let me know, and life is good."

"Got it."

"I'm afraid they will be on their own—lot of

ground to cover. So they won't be able to BS with each other. Like I just saw them doing."

"Right."

"One more thing, Mathews."

"Yes, Dr. Graulich?"

"If you feel, as the leader of this squad, that you need more marines out here on patrol while we set off explosives, while we dig—you just let me know?"

"I will."

Graulich smiled. She almost added, *Good boy.* "Glad we had this chat. Get to it."

18

"ALL RIGHT, MARINES—UM, SPACE MARINES— find any available seat and buckle in. If this is your first damn time riding an ion ship, get ready to suck wind!"

Kane looked around. About fifty marines, so young, stumbling into the ship. With seating for a hundred or so, finding a seat to himself wouldn't be a problem.

The seats, designed with all the attention to the comfort of its soldiers that the military was known for, didn't look much better than the seats on one of the big attack transports. Except these seats had three-way harnesses that—Kane imagined—would hold the passenger safely pinned to the seat even if the ion ship flipped upside down at five g's.

He looked behind the rows of seats and saw a

bulkhead with a door that he thought probably led to some kind of cargo area. And up front, what must be a VIP section.

Kane could hear the clanging and banging as heavy items got loaded into the belly and rear of the ship.

So this will get me to Mars, he thought. And though he had picked a seat way in the back where he thought he'd be alone, that plan didn't work. A scrawny kid looked at the seat next to Kane.

"This free?"

Kane nodded.

The new space marine stuffed his pack into the compartment above the seats. Despite the fact that these ships moved a lot of heavy equipment at minimal cost, space marines were restricted to only the most basic of personal goods. *You'll get everything you guys need up there.* The sergeant who'd said that had worn a real sick grin.

"Name's Tobias Mitchell Smith," Kane's seatmate said.

Kane looked at him, hoping his demeanor would inform the kid of his disinterest in any talk whatsoever. "Kane," he said.

"People call me 'Smitty.' Always have." The kid stuck out a hand.

Christ, Kane thought. *Gonna be a long trip to the Red Planet.*

"You ever . . . you ever ride in one of these things?"

Kane shook his head. *Maybe I should just tell him to shut . . . the hell . . . up.*

"Me either. Going to be something, I can't wait to—"

A soothing voice filled the transport. "Five minutes until launch initialization."

"Wow," Smitty said. "You know—Kane, is it? That your first name?"

Kane shook his head. "Kane will do."

"You know, I heard that the takeoff feels like you're in some kind of bullet. The whole ship tilting, rocketing up, before hitting orbit. And these seats, they—"

Enough. Kane looked at the kid, hoping that Smitty, probably fresh out of what used to be the farm belt and now *so* damn excited about going to Mars, might see that the person he was sitting next to wasn't exactly a newbie. That it was this or get executed. "Look, Smitty. Maybe we should just sit back, okay? And, you know, enjoy the goddamn launch." Kane kept his eyes on the kid. And finally a flash of recognition there: that maybe not bugging this guy would be a good thing.

"Yeah. Right. Just, you know, experience it."

Kane nodded.

"Launch initialization in one minute. System check begun. Harnesses locked. Cabin secure."

Kane didn't hear a click, but he imagined that the weblike straps now crossing his body could not be undone. He looked ahead. His hands closed on the thin armrest. And he had to admit that despite everything, he was looking forward to seeing what this ride was going to be like.

Kane knew almost nothing about the ion engine. But he did know that the engine would not even kick in until this transport was free of the atmosphere. And to get to that point would require the basic thrust of ordinary rocket power.

"Launch sequence initialized."

Kane felt the ship tilt back, and as it did, so did the rows of seats, now turning slowly, realigning themselves as the ship got into launch position.

"This is going to be something!" Smitty was getting excited.

The ship approached a near-ninety-degree position, and Kane heard his own seat row lock into position.

"Thrust sequence commenced."

The engines—a mere fifty meters behind them—kicked in, the roar deafening.

"Five seconds to launch . . . four . . . three . . . two . . ."

He looked at the kid next to him, grabbing the arms of his seat with all the power his scrawny arms could manage. Kane threw him a bone. "No need to hold on; the g's will keep you—"

Then the ship began to move. The interior cabin vibrated. Kane blinked as his eyes got used to the constant quivering. Already he felt the force pushing him back into the seat. And then, the speed started to build. Until Kane felt the massive g-force pressing against every inch of his body. He was glad he had skipped a big breakfast. And he hoped the kid next to him had also.

More force, and the sound of the engines deafening despite the baffles and thick acoustic tiles that covered the cabin.

Kane looked out the small porthole. Not much to see at first, save for the whitish gas of the atmosphere streaming around the ship as it rose.

In the old days this was probably where some of the thrusters would be jettisoned, dropping back to Earth for—with luck—reuse. But at least that part of this ancient science had improved. The engines were now more efficient, almost compact, the fuel cocktails designed for maximum power. But then the ship rolled a bit to the right, speeding north, and Kane got a glimpse of the Arctic—the bare patch surrounding the ice cap tightening, each year less ice during the winter until the Arctic Sea would turn into a year-round fishing ground. Until that too was tapped out.

Then, as the ship turned again, already close to deep space, he could see South America and the smoky, smudgy clouds dotting the continent. So many fires there, the rain forest burning away, and in Africa too, no way to contain them, so they just burned, gobbling up the forests like a beast, forever removing them from the planet. Nobody had been able to put a positive spin on that one.

"This is . . . so cool," Smitty said. Guess it was good the kid was enjoying himself. Kane would have just liked to get the dead weight of acceleration off his body.

Then he heard the recorded female voice: "Attaining Earth orbit in one minute." Another glance out the window. The white slipstream gave way to a startling clarity now, and Kane saw a lush purple sky. They were leaving the atmosphere, and only moments away from the vacuum of space.

Then: "Orbit attained."

Like a glider hitting the crest of its arc, then curving down, the ship began to slowly tilt. But this time there was little physical sensation. A click: the gimbal mechanism that controlled the seats released and they realigned themselves to their early horizontal position.

"Hey!" the kid tapped Kane. "Look at this, man!"

Kane looked out the port again. The sky dark, filled with stars. Dizzying with stars.

"Ain't that something?"

And Kane had to give the kid that—the view was spectacular.

Now for part two of the trip. "Switching to ion engines in five . . . four . . . three . . . two . . ."

The compact, powerful thrusters that got them to orbit flew away to the sides as the ship rode the orbit. Each thruster's own autopilot returned it to a landing spot below. Then a low level hum, almost soothing, filled the cabin as the recorded voice said, "One. Ion engines engaged."

Smitty's face was plastered against the small port, so Kane could see nothing.

"What happened?" Kane tapped the other marine's shoulder. "Let me see."

The beautiful space night, the lush dark sky dotted with millions of stars, had vanished. What Kane now saw was something he had never seen before, or could even describe. He wondered why there had never been any vids or pictures of *this?* Maybe because all personal cameras had to be stowed for launch for security reasons, they were told.

The traditional space sky had been replaced with something that looked like a net of curling light trails, all different colors, slowly bending, twisting. It was like being inside some kind of complex molecule from chemistry class, as though they had been shrunk.

"Where are we?" Smitty asked.

Kane didn't have a good answer to that one. And he knew now why pictures weren't allowed. Whatever those curling, coiling light trails were, they had something to do with how the UAC's Ion Engine worked. The view outside was the strangest and most beautiful thing John Kane had ever seen.

"We're in space, kiddo. Just . . . let it go."

The kid nodded. Kane leaned back in his seat and shut his eyes.

"Travel time to destination . . . fifty-one hours,

twenty-three minutes, and eighteen seconds." A trip that should take six months . . . now no more than two days. Two days, and then Mars would be outside the port.

The War Planet. A second Earth—if the UAC/USA propaganda was to be believed. A second homeland. *We'll see about that*, Kane thought. And with that last thought, he fell deeply and blissfully asleep.

19

DR. MALCOLM BETRUGER STOOD AT THE MAS-
sive window of his office that overlooked all of Delta.
From here he could see every part of the labs, save
for those specimen and equipment rooms that lined
the three corridors leading from the lab.

He looked down at all the scientists hurrying, pre-
paring things, and he thought: *Which one is it? Which
one of them is a traitor?*

One of them was sending information back to Kelliher. Betruger knew that simply from the messages
he'd received from Kelliher directly and the communications from his flunkies in the UAC. And not only
that, now two of Kelliher's key people were coming
back here, because Kelliher was "alarmed"—by what
was going on here in the lab.

A year of amazing discoveries, incredible events, and he was . . . *alarmed.*

Betruger, however, had already guessed early on that there was a spy. But no matter, he had started to change things long before that. Most of the scientists below thought that they were still trying to crack the problem of animate teleportation.

Missing the big idea completely.

A few—maybe—suspected that Betruger had lost interest in mere teleportation. They might have noticed that Betruger seemed preoccupied by something *else.* But if he confided in no one, then what proof would they have? Because as far as Betruger was concerned, these experiments, this lab, Mars itself—it wasn't about teleportation at all. He walked to his door and started down for the main floor of the lab.

Axelle Graulich ran her hand over a section of what looked like exposed metal that lined the cave wall. It all reminded her of *something.* The curves, the straight lines, some running straight then deeper right into unexposed sections of the cave. Other sections curled up to the ceiling.

A tech team of space marines recorded the outline and size of the newly exposed section.

What was it?

Most of her colleagues thought that these could be runes, but that was all. Reminders of the long-vanished Martian civilization. But then, Axelle had asked them, where was the fossil record? All this dig-ging, and no bones, nothing?

Her chief planetary climatologist, Dr. Paul Stifel, had an idea about that. Weather. "Fossilization re-quires special conditions, Axelle. Earth may be filled with fossils, but that's because Earth is—it appears—a special planet. Lots of water, lots of sediment, the lay-ers forming. Perfect to preserve a fossil record. Here, we don't have a clue what the planetary systems have been for the past million or two years."

That was true enough. In fact, they knew so little about Martian geological history that she assumed they were decades away from even having a theory about any Martian civilization and whatever catas-trophe had destroyed it. If that was indeed what hap-pened.

"Make sure you get detailed shots of those sec-tions above us!" she shouted to the techs recording all this. Again—as if on impulse—she reached up and touched another curving section, as if it somehow invited touch.

There was something else that bothered Axelle: Betruger. Months ago, after this major breakthrough on the site, he changed orders on how all the Site 3 information and data would be treated. Everything now went directly to Betruger.

And when they found an artifact, dubbed U1, it went immediately to Delta Lab and, Axelle guessed, Betruger's team. U1—looking partly like a shield, party like a sculpture, the material unknown, impervious to any traditional scans. And now, by his order, in Betruger's hands.

After that, Axelle didn't know who saw it. Whenever she raised the question with Betruger, he would turn on her as if she was challenging his authority.

"No, Dr. Betruger, I just—"

"You will follow the procedures I have outlined, Dr. Graulich. Or you can be reassigned."

The thought filled her with dread. The work at the site was amazing. To be removed now would be devastating.

She stepped back from the new opening in the ground.

"Axelle, can I tell the team they can press on?"

She turned to Tom Stein. He had been the first to question the new rules for processing information. Axelle tried to offer some arguments about security that she didn't believe in. Stein had countered them all, telling Axelle that she should go directly to General Hayden and complain. *Why does Betruger control everything we do here? Who knows what he's doing with the information?*

Who indeed? Not her, for sure.

"What's that, Tom?"

"I'd like them to start drilling down a bit farther. These things"—he raised a hand to one of the metallic squiggles—"seem to converge there. The one here looks different. They're changing as we expose more."

"Different? How?"

"Well, now they look almost like, well, arteries. They get thicker. And if they 'come' from anyplace, it's down there."

Arteries. That was an interesting view. And at least she didn't need Betruger's approval to carry on the work here. "Yeah—I think we have all this area documented. So slowly now . . . they can get back to the excavation."

"Great. I'll be watching and—"

"Right, but if these things do seem to converge, make sure the team takes extra care. If they are runes, if they do mean something, if there is a damn message in all this, we don't want to miss a piece that might turn out to be the Rosetta stone."

"You got it."

Stein walked away. She had noticed how the entire team seemed to work double time now, hurrying, cutting breaks short, not even wanting to go back to the city itself.

They want to stay here. Like I do.

Working away, opening more of the cave, the tunnels to the side, slowly, carefully bringing it back out into the Martian light. She took another look at the walls and ceiling.

Yes, like arteries. But also . . . like, what did they call them decades ago? Circuit boards. Like those old circuit boards in the museums. The squiggles connecting, separating. Arteries, circuits—or something else?

Time, she expected—hoped—would tell all.

• • •

MacDonald stood by Chamber B—the receiving chamber—as technicians continued to examine the large, clear chamber from inside and out. After what happened during the last test, the unit could have been damaged in a number of places.

"How's it looking?" he said to one of the men scanning the surface for any signs of cracks.

"So far, so good. Looks good as new."

MacDonald nodded. Not the answer he wanted. Better that it be damaged. Needing repair. Buy some time. As soon as Betruger announced another test, MacDonald hoped that something would be found to postpone it.

"Keep looking," he said. "You find anything—any damage at all—let me know."

He looked up to see Betruger walking down to the main lab floor.

That was another thing. Betruger had stopped talking to the team. Oh, he still gave orders, still told the team what to do, what was going to happen. But for anything else, Betruger was a closed book. MacDonald began to think; *Something is wrong with him.* The strain, the pressure—something—was making him snap.

He had tried to tell Kelliher that in his secret reports. But the UAC boss never came back asking for more details. *Maybe all Kelliher wants is for the damn thing to work.*

MacDonald felt someone touch his arm, surprising him. He turned around. "Ishii? What is it?"

He looked at Dr. Jonathan Ishii, the lead systems data analyst. He was the one person who knew as much as Betruger about what was really happening in the chambers.

"They got one!" Ishii whispered the words, but it was shrill, breathy, frantic.

"Easy. What do you mean?"

Ishii looked around. *We do that a lot lately*, MacDonald knew. *All of us. Looking around. Seeing if Betruger is watching us.* This place had become a paranoid's heaven.

Dr. Ishii leaned close. MacDonald could almost smell the man's fear. *The guy's going around the bend,* MacDonald thought. He'd best put a word in with the medical team. *Someone better have a look at him, and fast.* The psych team on Mars City was beginning to work overtime.

Another breathy whisper . . .

"They got another human volunteer. I've been told by Betruger. We test again in twenty-four hours."

Ishii grabbed MacDonald's arm. No one trusted anyone, and he certainly couldn't trust Ishii. "Okay, another test. Against my better judgment. Against yours too, maybe?"

Ishii's eyes widened. "But you don't get it! We can't let him do it."

"We can't stop it, Jonathan. Betruger runs the lab. If some poor marine—"

Ishii's eyes widened and darted right. MacDonald guessed that they soon wouldn't be alone.

Then Betruger was there.

"Dr. MacDonald, Dr. Ishii—all in good order here?"

MacDonald answered. "Everything's checking out, Dr. Betruger. No problems."

Ishii still hadn't said anything.

"And you've triple-checked all the data systems, Ishii?"

The other scientist nodded. He looked like a wreck. *Definitely have to get him to the medical team.*

"Good. I've set the time. For tomorrow. The new test." Betruger nodded, as if speaking the words to himself. "Twelve hundred MMT."

Ishii said something too low for either of them to hear.

Betruger, who wasn't afraid to use his squat bullish body to make a point, took a step toward Ishii. "What's that? What did you say, Ishii?"

"Midday. The—that's midday tomorrow."

Betruger hesitated, then MacDonald saw him smile.

"So it is. You'd best get to work. Not a lot of time, eh?" Then Betruger walked away. And when MacDonald turned back to Ishii, he too had hurried off.

And not for the first time MacDonald wondered: *Are we all going to lose it up here?*

20

IAN KELLIHER OPENED THE DOOR INSIDE HIS office. His personal assistant sat at a massive desk, just outside. One of two gatekeepers. Another receptionist sat at another desk beyond this room, controlling the electronic doors.

"Elaine, hold all calls and make sure that I'm not disturbed until you hear from me."

She looked up and smiled. "Yes, Mr. Kelliher." She was beautiful, but much more valuable as a trusted assistant than a potential mistress. Besides, he had plenty of those. Different women for different moods. All discreet and enamored of the power that being UAC head brought.

He shut the office door, hit a button, and his PDA screen projected itself into the air in the center of the room. "Stauf," he said. A code word. An anagram of his own choosing. And the secret cache of reports from Mars became available.

"Today. Play."

The screen showed Delta Lab, everyone ready for the test. Then he heard MacDonald's voice.

"Sir, as you can see, plans are going forward full speed for the new test. Betruger says he has his volunteer. Unconfirmed as yet, and Dr. Betruger is confiding in no one. But if you don't want this test to occur, I suggest you have only the next twenty-four hours to stop it. And as a reminder . . ."

Macdonald's transmission then showed the still images from the last human test, even more horrific when frozen. The poor volunteer hacking, coughing out his insides on the lab floor.

The images made Kelliher's stomach tighten. But the prize—you had to keep your eye on that. Though he appreciated MacDonald being his eyes and ears, Kelliher knew this: He had no intention whatsoever of stopping Betruger. Not when there were signs, re-assurances that this time, with the new calibrations, with new adjustments to the chamber's transmission systems, Betruger just might succeed.

Kelliher was willing to risk another experiment or two. Especially now that he would have his own people on site to shut it down.

Betruger's chances and days might indeed be numbered. But there was no need for the scientist to know that.

"Clear." Then: "Elaine—"

"Sir."

Kelliher walked around to his desk. "I'm open for business again."

"Yes, sir."

And during the day's affairs, the meetings needed to run the global empire that was UAC, Kelliher knew he'd only be half listening. Because he'd really be thinking about Mars, Betruger, and what was going to happen tomorrow.

21

MARIA STOOD IN THE BACK OF THE MEETING room in the center of Marine Headquarters. Sergeant Kelly had ordered all the grunts on duty for the next twelve hours to assemble. But so far he was just flipping through his screens.

Rodriguez leaned close. "Hey, did you hear who volunteered?"

"Let me guess. An idiot?"

Rodriguez laughed. Easily entertained, she knew. "Yeah, well, I almost did. Did you see the deal they're offering? Fantastic. Never have to do this shit again. No, it's that guy Wegner. Know him? Pretty quiet SOB. And man, he's got to be old. Maybe even thirty, thirty-five."

"Maybe that explains why—"

Kelly looked up and said, "Okay, listen up. Here's

what's going to happen." He closed the screens and put his hands on his hips, facing the two dozen marines standing in the room.

"We got a bunch of new jarheads landing in the next hour, and I've decided the best way to get these newbies all oriented to our lovely digs here is to assign each of you . . . one of them to babysit."

"Christ," said Maria. Bad enough she had been passed over for any grade advancements. No good deed went unpunished. But now this? Babysitting someone new? *Shit.*

"I'll make the assignments when they arrive. Can't get the damn roster on my PDA. But you know the drill. Get them outfitted. Weapons, supplies. Show them their quarters, give them the quick tour. No need for any monorail rides or treks to Delta, got it? And I want them by eighteen hundred to know this place as well as any of you screwups. Good. And oh yeah—I don't want them hearing about any stupid-ass rumors you guys talk about. That's the last sort of garbage they need. Okay. Make sure your own PDAs are updated with the latest schematics."

Maria saw a hand go up to her left.

"Right, Bloom—what the hell you want?"

"Any EVA, sir? Show them how to get to the Mars City egress points?"

Kelly paused. Something he hadn't thought about. Not the brightest bulb in the box, Maria knew. But not a bad sarge. Talked straight and didn't chew your ass unless you deserved it. "No. We don't have time for that. Got to get these guys into the rotation by tonight. So they'll have to figure that out on their own. Just—you know—show them what I told you. Okay, fall out."

The space marines started milling out of the room. Maria looked around, then grabbed Rodriguez's arm. "So this Wegner—he's gone already?"

Rodriguez took a look around. "I don't know. Maybe. I mean, he's in our detachment so he should be here. Maybe he gets like a last meal or something." Rodriguez leaned close. "Maybe some Martian poontang." The last joke sent Rodriguez into a tricky combination of snort-laughs.

Guy must really do well on first dates. "Right," Maria said.

Life on Mars—could it get any better?

22

JACK CAMPBELL TAPPED THE PORTHOLE WINDOW. "It's looking on schedule, Swann. The place is nearly done."

"Yeah—not without more money than budgeted, more people, more of the UAC's resources. Not that that concerns you."

Campbell nodded. "Right. It doesn't." He turned and looked at Swann. "You sure you're ready for what we have to do?"

Swann shook his head. "You know, I may not have had your training, I don't know ten different ways to kill someone with my thumb and index finger or any of that crap . . . but yeah, bring it on."

Campbell laughed. "I actually know more ways than that. But good to hear. Because if things don't work out, the next few days aren't going to be pretty."

"I just think that Kelliher should have given Hayden a heads-up about what this trip was really about."

"He doesn't trust him. You know he thinks that Hayden is in Betruger's pocket." Campbell turned back to the outside. Mars swung into full view now, filling the port window, the sun making it glow a brilliant, burnished red. "First we square away Hayden, then Betruger. We'll earn our money over the next few days."

"Right."

For a moment they sat there in silence. The interior of the VIP compartment filled with the reflected reddish glow.

"I just wish—I mean, I don't think this is going to be too easy. If we have to terminate Delta Lab . . ."

"Pulling the plug is never easy, Swann."

A soothing voice filled their cabin. "Mars orbit stabilized. Landing in five minutes. Safety harnesses will now lock into place."

Campbell heard the click, the criss-crossed straps again holding him tight to the seat.

"Cabin realignment sequence initiated."

Almost imperceptibly, the chairs in the cabin began gliding back as the *Darkstar* prepared to enter the Martian atmosphere.

Campbell looked at Swann again. "Just don't worry, Swann. It's all going to be fine."

And then the transport's thrusters fired, guiding the ship carefully into the Martian atmosphere and down to the main landing area of Mars City.

• • •

The ship touched down with the gentlest of bumps.

Pretty amazing, Kane thought. Something this large, and he barely felt anything. He heard a click; the harnesses released.

"Welcome to Mars City," the computer voice said.

"Cool," Smitty said. "This is something, hmm?"

Something? Kane had to wonder. He had just done a trip that humankind had dreamed about for centuries, so how come he felt no excitement, no anticipation, just . . . caution?

Some of the other space marines had started standing up, recovering their packs from the compartments above and below the seats.

Then Kane flashed on the possible source of his unease. From the beginning he had found this posting, this whole deal, odd. The UAC Mars City project was well known to be a dumping ground, at least if you were in the military. *But they wanted me up here for a reason. And nobody bothered to tell me what it was,* Kane thought.

He pulled himself out of the contoured seat, reached up, and grabbed his bag out of the now-open compartment. He started down the aisle to the exit, and at the same time noticed Smitty hurrying to stay up with him. *Guess I got myself a new friend,* Kane thought.

The exit ramp led to an enclosed area of the hangar. The landing system allowed for the hangar to open directly to the Martian atmosphere while pressure systems kept both temperature and air at livable levels.

As soon as a series of suspended lights at the top of the hangar showed green—meaning the hangar was sealed—crews came running out to begin unloading the transport. Kane looked over to the metal crates being quickly offloaded, recognizing the shape and size from his own supply runs.

Weapons. Quite a lot for a research facility.

Then he watched one of the robot off-loaders open another freight compartment in the ship's underbelly. And then it pulled out a really massive crate.

Now that's . . . a big gun.

Two guys in suits walked over to the pile of crates, like kids inspecting what Santa left under the tree. Heavy weapons, heavy UAC suits . . . *What's going on up here?*

One of the UAC men—stocky, looking like he could handle himself—crouched down and inspected the big metal case. Kane watched him slide his hand along the metal. *Must be nice to be in love.*

"Hey, you. Get over here with the others. Now!"

Kane whirled around to see a sergeant staring at him.

"Sure, Sergeant," he said. The sergeant kept eyeballing Kane as he walked back to the rest of the new arrivals.

"All right, new marines, fall in, two lines. You goof-offs have a busy Martian day ahead."

Marines . . . interesting. Kane wondered whether this guy had been recruited from the real marines and still couldn't get his tongue around that word, *space*.

The new arrivals fell into two lines, Kane near the middle. Some of them, like Smitty, so damn young. Just kids.

The sergeant said, "My name is Master Sergeant Kelly. My voice will be—for you—the voice of Mars. When I say 'move' up here, you damn well better move fast. The same rule applies to jumping, running and every other damn bodily function that you newbies can think of. Now you grunts—follow me."

The two lines of space marines walked behind Kelly past large doors and into an open room, which, Kane thought, looked surprisingly like the reception area of a sleek hotel.

"Welcome to Mars City," a woman sitting behind the reception desk said. Guess no one told her that you didn't have to actually *talk* to the jarheads.

Kane watched Kelly move fast, hurrying past the reception, into another large room, people moving quickly back and forth. *Certainly busy here.*

Then down a corridor to the left.

All resemblance to a hotel vanished as the corridor turned industrial, all massive tubes. *Obviously we're heading to the marine area.*

Kelly held up a small device—probably his PDA—and doors swung open, and then into a room where other marines stood waiting. Like an ambush, Kane thought. Big grins on their faces.

"All right. Hold it up here. These marines here, they're going to babysit you. You'll each have your own personal tour guide to show you the Mars City layout, get your gear sorted, weapons assigned, where you eat, sleep—and do the rest of your stuff. You got that?"

Kane looked over the group, all making comments to each other. Looking at the new meat. *This is gonna be fun*, he thought.

23

"WHERE IS HE?" SWANN SAID TO HAYDEN.

"Keep your pants on, counselor. Dr. Betruger has been sent for; he knows you're coming, and you can just be patient."

Swann noticed how different Hayden's tone was without Kelliher at the meeting. Hayden made no secret of hiding his disgust.

But then Campbell—sitting in a chair, looking at a table screen now synced to his PDA—spoke up. "You sure you understand the seriousness of this, General? Do you understand what's at stake?"

"I sure the hell do. I don't need any reminders from you two."

"There are," Swann said, "liabilities. Things that could hurt the UAC. And we must make sure Betruger understands."

That prompted a small laugh from Hayden, who walked over to Swann. "You think . . . do you *really* think that after letting Dr. Betruger have control, complete control, that now you can—what—pull the reins in?"

"That's what we're here for. Especially if the new tests fail."

Hayden looked from Swann to Campbell. "Well, good goddamned luck."

Dr. Jonathan Ishii opened the file only two people in all of Mars City were permitted to see. He looked around to be sure that nobody stood around his workstation.

One file was filled with all that imagery that had started pouring from Site 3. From the start, Betruger wanted to control who had access to it. In fact, for the time being he wanted only two people seeing it, he said. Two people analyzing it.

So while the field team out at the site thought that a matching team was analyzing the information back in Delta, the truth was far from that.

Ishii licked his lips. Always so damn dry. Why was that? No sleep, dry lips, and Ishii knew that something was wrong with his heart rate. He could almost feel it, now fast, now slowing, as if someone was controlling it.

And though Ishii was the lead data analyst, there were many other people who could help analyze all this stuff, compare it to any known symbols, to identifiable runes—put everything found through so many filters and data systems. Wasn't that the way things were supposed to be done?

There . . . just now! His heart sped up. Because he was thinking about his plans. Because he had thoughts that he wasn't telling anyone else. Or maybe . . . maybe because he thought someone could read those thoughts. See them.

Did Betruger know what Ishii was planning?

His hand passed over the screen. And there—in such clear three-dimensional images that he could almost touch them—the sections of the wall, the curling lines, the odd shapes found at Site 3. All meaningless when you were working to expose them, following that trail of bread crumbs. But not meaningless to Ishii or Betruger.

The symbols soon resolved themselves into an icon-based system. And though Ishii had only scratched the surface of the meaning of most of the symbols, he now knew a few things. Things he told Betruger and no one else.

In fact, Betruger had ordered Ishii to tell no one. Betruger, leaning over him, that massive head, thin lips, his eyes boring into him, *Tell no one, Ishii, No . . . one.*

Symbols that spoke of a civilization. Those who made the symbols also made this tunnel. Long gone, all vanished. Leaving no fossil record. And the first symbols about an adversary. Yes, something indicating an *enemy*. As data searches scoured every symbol-based language from cultures dating from tens of thousand of years ago, the image, the idea . . . of "an enemy."

He couldn't be sure—not at first. But there seemed to have been . . . a conflict . . . a battle . . . a war. So many of the symbols still to be deciphered.

Then something else that, at first, meant nothing. U1. The artifact. No ID tags from any of the databases popped up pointing to a likely interpretation.

Ishii twisted the image in every direction, turning it, looking at it. The artifact occupied an important place in the iconography of the walls. Twisting the image, turning it, until Ishii could feel that, yes, he was playing with it. Fascinated with it. This . . . device . . . or sculpture. . . .

Discovered at the entrance to the interior tunnel. So important. Everything else seemingly flowing around it, and its image and shape also found on the walls.

Ishii turned away, the strange image frozen at an odd angle. He looked away. Still no one watched him.

These scientists working here, doing the experiments, unaware of what he and Dr. Betruger were seeing, learning. He looked back, half expecting that the still image might move, might leap right off the screen, might grow and fill this room. Ishii kept looking at it. His heart raced even faster, a tear gathered in one eye. Fear, confusion? He didn't know.

He thought of his plan. Tomorrow. There would be

a chance tomorrow. When everyone was busy with the experiment. When everyone, even Betruger, would be occupied. That's when it would happen. Ishii quickly shut his screen off. Betruger had stood outside the door to the conference room. He couldn't hear anything being said within. No matter—he could easily guess what they were talking about, what they were arguing about.

He knew that Kelliher was growing more concerned. Concerned enough to maybe even shut the experiments down. Betruger imagined that there might be something planned. Not that he would ever allow it to happen. Not now that he knew what was *really* going on here. No, closing Delta down was simply unthinkable. But for now, he would humor them.

He opened the door.

Swann stopped in mid-sentence.

"Dr. Betruger—"

"Mr. Swann, Mr. Campbell . . ." Then Swann saw how Betruger barely hid his disgust. "General."

"Good to see you, Doctor," Campbell said.

Betruger nodded. "So to what do I owe the pleasure? And the interruption, I must say."

Campbell and Hayden looked in Swann's direction. *Great,* Swann thought, *let the bastard get mad at me.* "There have been new concerns raised, Dr. Betruger." Nothing from Betruger, so Swann continued. "Serious concerns about the results of the experiments. Security has become an issue. How long can we keep a lid on what's happening here? And are there any signs of progress? Mr. Kelliher has been considering—"

Now Betruger put up a hand. And Swann noticed that, for a scientist, Betruger was sturdily built. His hands were massive.

"You can hold it right there, Mr. Swann." He turned to the others. "No one will be closing this project. Has Kelliher forgotten what I have already created for him? And that's nothing—absolutely nothing—compared to what will come."

By now Betruger had both of his massive hands in front of him as if twisting and ripping something apart. *Like my neck,* Swann thought.

Campbell shook his head. He knew that the security head thought that all of Delta should have been shuttered months ago. "Dr. Betruger, I didn't say we were closing the lab. But we have to look at whether a hiatus might not—"

Betruger let his hands fall to his sides, suddenly pulling back from his midair mayhem. "Oh. A *hiatus*. A pause?" That idea wasn't sitting too well either. "Gentlemen, I know you serve at Mr. Kelliher's pleasure—" Didn't sound like he put himself in that same category. "—and I understand Ian's concerns. I would have the same concerns. So I therefore have a proposal for you to relay directly to Mr. Kelliher."

Something about this worried Swann. All of sudden Betruger was acting compliant, almost reasonable. It didn't make any sense.

"There is a new experiment scheduled for tomorrow . . ."

Swann cleared his throat. "With a volunteer?"

"Yes."

"I don't think we can. More animal tests, yes, but—"

Betruger smiled. "I am suggesting—*offering*—that you all come to Delta to witness the experiment. I am sure that what you will see will reassure you completely. I've scheduled it for noon."

"But it's the human volunteer aspect that has Mr. Kelliher so—"

"I know, I know—worried about the human subjects. What's happened so far, yes. As if they have any value compared to the prize."

"It could never happen on Earth, Doctor. And the UAC is moving to a 'one world' policy—"

"Earth, hm? Policies? We *are* on Mars, Swann. In case you haven't noticed. But still, if you come to the lab tomorrow, as my special guests, you will see that all of your fears—all of Mr. Kelliher's fears—are totally misplaced." He paused. "Do we have a deal?"

Something about the way he said *deal* . . .

"I will have to check with Mr. Kelliher."

"And with your support, he will agree. And then you, all of us, will see that we have absolutely nothing to be concerned about. Nothing at all."

For a moment nobody said anything. Swann

knew that Kelliher would, based on Betruger's word, permit one more human experiment. After all, the secret teams in Palo Alto were trying to find out exactly what was going wrong with the Martian transporters. He'd want all the information he could get.

"I'll contact Mr. Kelliher now."

"Very good."

Smiles all around.

"And I will see you gentlemen tomorrow. You will be amazingly surprised, I do believe."

With that Betruger moved to the door, almost rushing, impatient as it slid open. Then he was gone.

Campbell stood up. "How do you spell *bonkers?*" Nobody laughed. Then he added, "I'm going to check that they got the weapon crates in place . . . and also check on my baby."

Then Campbell sailed out.

Hayden looked up at Swann. "Baby? What the hell is Campbell talking about?"

"Security stuff, General. Wish I could tell you . . . but I can't."

Then Swann walked out, the air having grown too cold, too dry in the bright conference room.

24

KANE SAW A WARRANT OFFICER WALK OVER TO Kelly and pull him aside.

And for a moment the newbies and their guides-to-be were on their own. A few of them talked, the guides eyeing the new arrivals with unhidden disgust. *Same as it ever was,* Kane thought.

But then he noticed one of the jarheads who seemed to have locked his eyes on Kane. Kane met his gaze. Usually enough to make the other person look away. But not this guy. In a way that felt quite normal, Kane took the measure of the man. Big, maybe as tall as he was, six-foot-two, maybe bigger. A shaved head that made the shape of his cranium look like some kind of strange planet.

Kane knew this was trouble.

"Well, look at what the hell they have sent up to us."

The man didn't move. But now, with Kane knowing he was being addressed, he kept his eyes on the other space marine.

"If it isn't . . . Killer Kane."

The other marines looked at the man talking. Most seemed confused, not knowing what the guy was talking about. But Kane could guess.

"Yes, boys and girls, we have the honor of having a genuine marine killer in our midst. How many marines died, Killer Kane, because you couldn't obey orders?"

The man spit. An action, in these glistening confines, whose message was clear. It was a challenge.

"Hey, Kolski, ease up, man."

Kolski. Kane's bald-headed adversary now had a name. With Kelly gone, the kids were free to play.

Kolski took a step.

"Isn't that right, Killer Kane? Men died, and you're the one that made it happen. Oh, and are you enjoying being a private? You're lucky—" Another step. "We all hoped they'd kill your ass."

By now some of the other marines had fallen in behind Kolski, either intrigued by what was going to happen or just wanting to stay well away.

Kane slowly straightened up. His eyes went to Kolski's sidearms, twin handguns. Reminding Kane that he stood there, his pack beside him as if he was a little kid going to camp.

Kolski took another step. His face only inches away from Kane's.

"So tell us, Killer Kane. How many of *us* are you going to kill up here?"

And for the first time, Kane looked away from the dark eyeballs of the man in front of him.

He knew that Kolski watched him break eye contact. He knew, in fact, that Kolski's eyes would then also wander, drawn by curiosity to see where Kane looked.

Which was when Kane grabbed Kolski's throat. His hand tightened around the man's neck. He could—with enough pressure—kill him: cut off air, close the carotid artery—a half-dozen ways to make this man taunting him dead.

The marines behind Kolski stepped back.

"You should learn not to run off your mouth about things you know nothing about . . ." Kane looked at the single stripe on his sleeve. "Private Kolski."

Kolski's hand went for his gun. *Guess this guy really is crazy,* Kane thought.

Kane's other hand shot to the man's wrist before the holster was even unbuckled. He took the wrist and gave it a sharp turn to the left. Amazingly painful, but not so bad that Kolski wouldn't be able to use the hand again.

Already Kane was doing damage control on what he was doing here. But this was necessary if he wanted to survive up here. Still, there would be some fallout, and it wouldn't be good.

The man's wrist freed, Kane's left hand grabbed at the guy's midsection and now, using his two hands like pincers, he pivoted the now bug-eyed Kolski backward, pointed to the ground where he landed with a thwack that ensured his head would be hurting for the next few days.

"So, you just better . . . shut . . . the hell . . . up."

Kane was about to release Kolski and back off. But he felt two massive hands yank him backward. "What the hell you doing, Private?" Kelly had ripped Kane back, and now, with surprising strength, threw Kane against the wall.

Now it was Kane's turn to land against hard stone. He saw Kelly look at Kane's nametag.

"Kane. Shit . . ." The sergeant said the name slowly, with understanding. "Moraetes, get over here."

Kane watched one of the female marines walk out of the pack and toward the sergeant. Short for a marine, Kane thought. For a moment her dark eyes fell on Kane. Then they rolled away. She didn't seem exactly thrilled at what was about to happen.

"Moraetes, this one's yours. Make sure that this newbie with a short fuse knows this place like the back of his palm. Oh, while you're at it, maybe you can teach him something about not doing anything impulsive."

The others laughed. Some kind of inside joke?

Moraetes stood by Kane and said nothing.

"Okay, let's get the rest of you paired up with your

own goddamn babysitters. And then start the grand tour . . ."

The marine, Private Maria Moraetes, stood beside Kane, silent as they waited in line for Kane to get his gear from Combat Prep. Finally Kane spoke. "You don't have much to say."

She looked at him. "No, I don't."

More seconds, and then Kane stood before a desk. A standard-issue pistol and holster were slapped down, looking a little frayed at the edges. *How low the mighty have fallen.*

Maximum ammo 360 rounds, clip capacity 12—not exactly a high-tech weapon. He turned back to his keeper.

"This the best firepower they've got up here?"

"There are rocket launchers, plasma guns, shotguns—the usual. But why the hell would we need them up here?"

The marine behind the desk put down a PDA. That at least looked state-of-the-art. A pile of fatigues, and then a key card.

"Feels almost like Christmas."

"Right," Moraetes said. "Okay, there's a video in your PDA—welcome to Mars and all that crap. You can watch that later. Let me show you your bunk. Then the tour, and I can be all done with you."

"I can feel your enthusiasm."

•   •   •

Kane followed Moraetes out of the hivelike bivouac that provided narrow bunks for a few dozen marines. Not much privacy.

He hurried to keep up with Moraetes as she walked out of Marine Command, heading back to reception.

"You got maps in the PDA that will always let you know where you are, and how to get from one place or another. Even"—another glance—"an idiot could do it."

"Then I should be just fine."

"But if Kelly wants you to get a tour, then that's what you get. We're heading back to the Command Access Junction, then I'll show you the main arteries of Mars City . . . and the underground."

"Right."

Other marines, some of them new arrivals, passed them. Seemed to be a lot of marines up here for what was supposed to be a civilian project.

"There are other access points, but this is the main one that brings you—"

Kane heard a scream. No, he thought, more of wail. Someone moaning. Moraetes stopped—they stood outside a room marked "All-Faith Chapel."

Another loud wail, then words . . .

"No, no . . . I can't. I can't do that, please don't make me—" Then the voice trailed off into sobs; more inchoate wailing.

"Someone's having a bad day . . ." Kane said.

Then two marines in armor, followed by someone in white, ran into the chapel.

"There goes another one."

Kane turned to her. "Another one? Another what?"

Now a true raging scream from inside, the man at full volume: "Stay away. Stay . . . away! I know they sent you. But it's too late. Too late, that's the thing, nobody—"

Kane took a step toward the entrance.

"I don't think you should—" Moraetes started to say.

But then Kane went in there, looking in.

The man had backed up to a generic altar. He held a gun. Spittle flew from his mouth as he raged. "You can't take me. They won't let you. Don't try."

The two marine security guards had moved to either side of the man, flanking him. Classic strategy, make the crazy man look left and right. They barely moved—waiting. But Kane imagined they would close in soon.

"They'll take all of us, you know. Every single one of—"

Then the marine on the right moved, bringing his pistol down on the man's hand. The screamer's gun fell to the floor, and then the marines moved fast to pin the screamer against the altar, then onto it. Looking almost like a human sacrifice. And the doctor hurried now, an injection gun in his hand. In seconds it was over.

One of the marines turned to see Kane at the doorway. "What the hell are you lookin' at?"

Kane nodded and walked away. Enough trouble for one day.

"Come on, Kane," Moraetes said. "Show's over."

The elevator door opened. They faced a sign that read, "Welcome to the Space Marines."

Except someone had crossed out *Space Marines* and replaced it with a single word.

Doom.

"Morale a little low up here?"

"Morale's fine. Couldn't be better."

"Yeah, I can see that."

Moraetes hurried past an underground security desk. "Down here you're about to walk through the guts of Mars City. The main convergence chamber is down here, then maintenance, and one of the major energy processing plants. If you head that way—a long way—you get to the old communications station. They're going to do something with it eventually, but for now—"

Kane grabbed his guide.

"Hold on." Two marines walked down the hallway, slowly talking.

Kane waited until they passed. "Enough with the hallways and big machines that I don't give a damn about what the hell they do. I have some questions."

Maria stood there, listening.

"Can you find some place where we won't have people walking by every minute?"

Moraetes looked up at him. For the first time he

got a good look at her face. He could see that her dark eyes were matched with wisps of jet-black hair under a fatigue cap. Then, because he was only human, his eyes trailed to her lips. But he brought his eyes back to hers, hopefully before she noticed.

"Questions. All right, I *am* your babysitter. Guess I can handle a few questions. There are some quiet areas past Energy Processing, storage, places where they dump equipment." She smiled, her first. "All part of the tour. Come on . . ."

Moraetes led Kane down a curved passageway, then cut down another tunnel-like hall.

"A guy could get lost down here."

She stopped and turned to him. "And this isn't even the half of it. They've just finished a new wing that connects to Delta, so besides the monorail—"

"Delta?"

She laughed. "Watch your damn briefings on the PDA, okay? Delta. The massive experimental lab that—my guess—is the real reason everyone is really up here."

"And in Delta they do . . . ?"

"Who knows. They're not telling us, that's for sure."

Kane thought of the crates he saw being unloaded. Lot of firepower for a peaceful outpost.

"You said you had some questions?"

"I think I started. But first, why did Kelly assign you to me. His crack about . . . being impulsive?"

Maria grinned. "Guess he thought I might be—what's the word—*simpatico.*"

"How's that?"

"I saved Kelliher's life nearly a year ago."

"And that's a bad thing?"

"Guess they thought I was impulsive, risked getting him killed. But I knew I could take the guy out who held him hostage. So I did."

"Where does that confidence come from?"

She looked up to Kane, her eyes locked on his. For a moment, the intensity was almost too much. *Been a while*, Kane thought. Too long. Best keep this aboveboard.

"I used to fight. Professionally."

He laughed. "What?"

She smiled, not annoyed at his laugh. "On Earth. Lightweight boxer. Number three contender. Fought all over." She took a step closer, and now it was definitely too intense. "I was good. Fast."

"Boxing. How do you get into—"

"You get into it when you have nothing else. My father died in the South African war—or whatever the hell they called *that* massacre. The government gave my mother nothing. Hardly any support. And somehow . . . I found I could hit. And move. And when I worked on it, I only got better."

"I'll have to remember that."

Then a full grin from her. "You do that, Kane."

"Okay. Explains why Kelly assigned you to me—or vice versa. Now, what was with that guy freaking in the chapel? That sort of stuff go on here a lot?"

Now Moraetes looked down the hall. Still quiet. Nonetheless, she lowered her voice. "Lot of weird stuff going down. Guys like that, freaking, dragged away. We get a few every week."

"And the cause?"

Moraetes gave him another smile. "You do ask a lot of questions."

"I like to know what kind of shit storm I'm walking into."

"Nobody knows. Some of them have worked in Delta, others not. All of them go completely paranoid. Babbling weird stuff . . . about *them*. How *they're* coming. How we can't do anything about it."

Kane looked away. The crates, his being sent up here . . . It started to make some sense. "I'm guessing," he said, "that there's a hell of a lot that they're not telling people up here."

"Got that right."

He reached out and put a hand on her shoulder. For a minute he thought she might shrug it off. There was a line between marines of the opposite sex. It was all about being a marine and nothing else. "Look, thanks for telling me this. I may have more questions." He tapped his PDA and smiled. "After I check out my videos."

"I'll be here. Got another year before I can get off this chunk of red rock."

"But I want you to know. You get in a jam. You need any help. I'm here too."

The classic deal. I got your back, and you mine.

She nodded. "Good. I'll remember that. Best we finish the damn tour, and then you can start your homework. Oh, and they do feed you up here."

"Glad to hear it."

Moraetes grinned and turned away, leading Kane to the main walkway and the secondary lift that would bring them back up to Central Access.

Kane gave her a nod and headed down to the marine bunks. She didn't mention it to him, but she knew his story. The marines killed, the rescue that didn't happen. But enough jarheads survived so that the true story got out. How the brass was willing to sacrifice a company, let them get wiped out—and Kane said no.

And sure, a lot of guys got killed. But he got a lot of guys out. And now he was here. They could have locked him up forever, even executed him. But they sent him here. Now why in the world would they do that?

She turned and went to Marine Command, and the start of her regular patrol.

25

"AXELLE, SHALL WE HOLD UP ON THE DRILLING?"

The scientist stood over the mammoth opening that, as far as she could tell, just kept going deeper, the symbols and intersecting patterns of the cave converging, dividing, and—as the pit went deeper—they seemed to change.

One thing she was sure of: this pit was no natural phenomenon. It had been made by something. But who, what—and where the hell were they? No bones, no record?

"I think I better go down, Tom. You stay here, and I'll go take a look. Tell them up front to hold off bringing any more explosives in."

Without damaging the sides of the giant pit, the team had carefully placed hand- and footholds, taking care to find unmarked areas to fasten the steps.

She turned around and started down, alone, into the pit.

The micro-exposives they had been using worked well, sending perfectly calibrated shocks into the Martian rock, shattering it like crystal. So far not a section of the pit wall had been damaged.

Hand over foot, moving slowly, the suit making the going cumbersome as Axelle headed down.

She felt a chill. Impossible, of course. Her suit regulated her temperature. The material, a mesh of micro-metals and a new plasticlike compound, was thin, but it could keep its wearer at a comfortable seventy-two degrees.

But as she went down, she thought, *It could be something else.*

And what's that? she asked herself. *What kind of chill is that?* Maybe the same one from her home in Wisconsin, when the power would go out . . . and the things in her room all started to take shape, change, transform . . .

She pushed the memory away.

But she did look up. The opening at the top of the pit made a perfect circle. What made this hole? And the veinlike protrusions on the side? Decorative, functional, symbolic, or—?

She hit the bottom of the pit. She checked in with Tom Stein.

"Does it look okay?" Tom asked. "Think we can keep going? That is—"

But another voice crackled in Axelle's ear. "Dr. Graulich."

Matt, the lead geologist, out at the cave opening.

"Yes?"

"We just got an alert from the weather satellite. Something in the East, coming fast."

She looked at the pit bottom, the handholds leading up. "I think I better get out of here."

But with another crackle in her ears, she knew she had said those words too late.

The doctor walked into the small medical cubicle and, without looking down, started examining the screens positioned right above the bed.

PFC Tom Wegner decided to crack a joke. "I'm gonna live, Doc?"

But the medical doctor didn't even smile. He just kept checking the readouts, tapping into his PDA.

"That bad, huh?"

Finally the doctor looked down. "No, son, it all looks good." Then the merest sliver of eye contact. "Just a few more minutes and we'll get you unplugged here . . . and I'll send the report to Dr. Betruger."

"I mean it all looks good, doesn't it? Nothing wrong that would keep me from the program?"

Wegner knew some of his fellow jarheads thought he was crazy to be volunteering. After all, had any of the other volunteers returned to duty? There were all those weird rumors. But there were always rumors in the military.

So some of those experiments didn't turn out so good. Maybe a few guys got hurt, sent home. But the rewards? Unbelievable. Could set yourself up for life with that amount of money. Immediate transfer to Earth, a cushy job, and cash. Pretty sweet deal.

And though Wegner didn't have a clue what the experiment involved, he didn't really care. Optimism—always a Wegner trademark. Gotta be optimistic these days.

"Okay, there we are. All done. Nurse—" A young nurse came in, a real cute one too, not one of the usual wrestler-types with full mustaches. She smiled at Wegner. "You can take everything off and"—now another glance at Wegner—"I'll tell Betruger you're all set. You'll sleep here tonight. Want you well rested."

Wegner fired a quick glance at the nurse. Maybe a guy could get lucky in the infirmary. A small smile from the nurse—as if she could read his mind.

"Great. I'll get a good night's sleep for a change. None of the other guys snoring away, huh?"

No response to that. And with a tug, the nurse pulled off the last wire that fed data into the monitors surrounding the bed.

To the nurse: "How are the eats in here?"

But the doctor answered. "You'll get a good meal."

Wegner grinned. Sounded good. Except—a good meal. *Isn't that what they do to guys about to be offed? A good last meal?* He let the thought move on. Optimism. Couldn't do much these days without a whole hell of a lot of that.

Billy Suppa, the marine guard on top of Ridge 93—all the big outcrops of rock were numbered—watched the storm approaching.

He had seen these dust devils before. The training vids showed them, and they also showed the damage they could do. Some kind of strange Martian weather phenomenon. Dust storms that sprang from nowhere and then began rolling across the red ground. Kind of like tornadoes, but shaped like a wave, always breaking, then reforming. Except—he hadn't seen one this big. Or this fast.

Billy could see two of the other marines arrayed on other ridges around Site 3. They had also turned to watch the zigzagging march of the storm.

"Got a big one coming," he said. Comm would pick up his comment to them, but that was okay. The no-chatter rule didn't apply to reporting something like this.

"Maybe we better—" he started to say.

But then he turned back to look at the two nearby marines.

One was gone. One minute there, and the next *gone*. Damn, that was fast. The other was still there, looking at the storm. Then he watched that guard vanish too, as if a hole had opened up beneath his feet.

Then Billy felt a rumbling beneath his feet. What the hell was this? The storm, now some ground tremor. And now—his eyes off the storm, looking down at the rocky jumble of stone he stood on—he felt movement.

A slow rumbling that quickly changed as a hole opened up right where he stood.

Billy started to send out a message. "Shit, something—"

But then he and the rest of his message vanished down a hole that just suddenly appeared.

Through the violent shaking, Axelle tried to hold on to the wall, to the handrails placed there by her team. They had been working this area for over a year, and never a tremor. Now, with the dust storm already scouring the ground around the cave opening, tossing their equipment all over the place, smashing it against the rock, they were in the middle of . . . what? A quake?

"Secure all the equipment," she said. "Tom . . . Tom, if you hear me, bring everything into the interior. We got—"

Then she could tell that her radio wasn't working. No sound from her earpiece. Totally dead. Some side effect of the storm?

"Anyone hear me? Anyone getting this?"

And as she held on to the handrail, she looked at the cave walls. The twirling, twisting mesh of raised lines and shapes began—ever so slowly—to glow. As if somehow, somewhere a power switch had been thrown.

Axelle grabbed the handrail tighter. And she tried to tell herself—to convince herself—that she wasn't scared.

"Got to go to work."

"Right. Thanks for the tour, Private Moraetes."

She smiled at Kane. "Maria. You can call me, Maria."

"Name works for me."

"And you?"

"Always been just Kane. So that will do."

Another grin. "Go do your homework, Kane."

He nodded, and started for his barracks.

Kane walked past Reception. Some people probably could be easily confused by the sprawling layout of this so-called Mars City. But when you'd spent as much time as he had fighting your way in and out of streets, past rubble, into landscapes where you damn well better know one rock from another—this was a piece of cake.

He saw a family. For a second he stopped. A man, his arm around a woman, holding a young boy's hand. Like they were taking a walk in the park. The guy's family must have arrived on the transport. Kane knew that some families actually lived here, the spouses and children of scientists and key administration people who didn't want to be separated for a year. Some promotional material back on Earth called them the first Martian homesteaders—though how anyone could consider living in these tunnels and halls homesteading, defied all logic.

The boy turned and saw Kane standing there. The father turned also.

The boy's eyes on him, Kane smiled. A kid, here. Seemed surreal. Kane nodded at the father, then started away.

But as he started moving toward his barracks, he heard the boy ask a question. "Daddy, why are there so many soldiers here?"

26

KANE PUT DOWN HIS TRAY OF FOOD, HAVING selected a table where only a few solitary jarheads ate. He hoped that he radiated the strong wish not to be bothered, until Smitty and another new marine from the transport came over.

"Hey, Kane—mind if we join you?"

Kane looked up. Perhaps this was the worst part of his punishment for his Terekstan breakout. He had to treat these clowns as equals. He nodded, and then speared something that looked like meat, but which he knew could not possibly be anything that had ever sprung from something alive.

"Did you see the size of this place? Man . . ."

Another nod. Probably all the encouragement that Private Tobias Smith needed. "It's kinda weird here, don't you think?"

Kane looked up. "Weird?"

"Yeah. I mean people seem jumpy. Like something happened, or is gonna happen." Smitty leaned close. "I saw someone who looked like they just lost it. *Snapped.* Some guards dragged this guy away. It just looked, I dunno—"

"Weird?"

Smitty nodded, and Kane took a sip of some lemony drink. Had to be a way to get a real drink up here. That might be worth exploring—

Then he heard a voice from behind. "Get all your homework done?"

He turned and saw Maria. Kane smiled—guess he didn't want to repel everyone here.

"Have a seat."

"I wish. Ate already, and I have to do one more circuit in Alpha."

"I'm supposed to finish getting this place locked into my head. So I guess . . . more vids, more maps—"

She smiled. "They'll put you to work tomorrow. Wish I could say that it will be exciting."

Smitty cleared his throat. "Hey, you've been here awhile, huh?"

Maria looked down at the newbie. She shifted her tone. Not a lady to annoy. "Yeah. So?"

"Um, what's up with everyone here? Like they're all tense and stuff."

Maria nodded. "Well, you see, that's because—" She leaned close, and her left side brushed Kane's shoulder. Touched, and stayed there a moment. "That's because"—she looked at the guy's name tag—"they're real tense . . . and stuff."

Kane laughed.

Then she pulled away.

"If I don't see you in the a.m.," she said, "be careful your first day. Big place, you know."

"Got it. And thanks."

She nodded, smiled, then turned away.

"Wow. She's something," Smitty said.

Kane didn't confirm or deny. He just went back to his meal, eager to hurry up and finish it.

Hayden's PDA made a small trilling noise, then a transparent screen appeared above his desk. An ID at the bottom identified the message as coming from the Comm Center. He recognized the face of the marine lieutenant but didn't know his name.

He touched a space on the floating screen, and the name appeared. *Lieutenant Hiram Kohl.*

"Lieutenant Kohl, what's up?"

"General, we have a major dust storm that moved across Ridge 93 and hit Site 3."

"And?"

"We've lost all communications."

"Right. Okay, but those sandstorms can do that, right? That happens?"

"Yes, sir."

"And is the storm still out there?"

"Yes, sir. The weather sat shows it kind of swirling around the area, just sort of waiting, even building a bit."

"Okay. Then that explains the communications drop."

"Sir, do you want to send a team out there?"

"No. Not with a storm still running around the area. They have plenty of air reserves, right? And when it's gone, I'm sure we'll hear from Graulich and her team."

"Should I inform Dr. Betruger?"

Hayden hesitated. Tricky one, that. Betruger could easily go nuts if he wasn't told what was happening.

"Um, let me do it." Hayden wanted to just get through the next twenty-four hours, the new experiment, with everything turning out just fine.

"Yes, sir. And shall I update you about—"

"Only if something is happening that requires my attention." He took a breath. "And that doesn't include dust storms. I can check the situation tomorrow."

"Yes, sir."

Hayden put his hand to the screen image floating in front of him, and the transmission ended. Twenty-four hours. A good experiment result. That was all he needed, and Mars could return to normal. He laughed to himself at that.

Kane looked at the small PDA screen, listening to Ian Kelliher talk.

"And this is just the beginning. What was once a base, a remote outpost on a distant planet, has started becoming a city of the future. Already people have started new lives, living on this new world. As the UAC, in partnership with your government, starts putting more resources into this great project, these new 'settlers' will be able to look forward to a future where they will grow their own food, produce all their own energy, and even mine the planet for resources.

"The dream of a Mars restored to being a living planet is not too long in the future at all. So join us, as we create the dream that is, and will be, Mars City."

Great, Kane thought. *Has me all excited.* From what he saw, Mars City, so far, appeared to be a series of massive bunkers, tunnels, and corridors sunken into the Martian ground. No playgrounds going up yet.

He flipped to one of the other vids, "Inside the Hydrocon."

"For centuries, people on Earth have waged war over two things vital to human existence—fuel and water. As part of its ongoing commitment to creating safer worlds for everyone, the UAC recently unveiled its development on Mars City of . . . the Hydrocon. The Hydrocon, though still in early experimental use on Mars, will, in one dramatic move, forever end all shortages of water and fuel.

"By splitting iron oxide molecules, the Hydrocon produces oxygen and hydrogen cheaply and safely without the need for large amounts of electricity. The hydrogen is then used for—"

He stopped that one. Unless Kelly had a quiz in his back pocket, he had seen enough for now. He put his PDA on the bunk beside him. He could hear the chatter of other marines. No matter. When you were this exhausted, you could sleep through a circus.

Betruger lay in bed, too anxious to sleep. *Tomorrow*, he kept thinking. Not even one more full day. *Tomorrow, and everything changes. The suits from Earth, Hayden, the marines here—everything changes for them.*

Sheer adrenaline could keep him going for days. Maybe sleep wasn't even needed at all anymore. But for this last night . . .

He needed to once more shut his eyes. To let the images come, the dreams, the—

(Instructions.)

So he paced his breathing. In, and out. Counting each breath. Clearing his mind until, in the quiet of his expansive room, off to the side of Delta, he fell asleep.

And they were there, waiting. At first, Betruger could just see the cave. No, not a cave. This was the gate, the true entrance, sealed so long ago.

When he first started having the dreams—what he then called "dreams"—he just thought that the results of the experiments must be getting to him. He was—he admitted in his personal journal—even a bit scared.

After all, he started walking through that cave, the walls alive, things moving on them, like blood-red vines shifting, changing, coiling—all in response to his steps. Like now. Only now he knew what was ahead, the fear long gone.

After all, he thought, *you can't be afraid of yourself, can you?* That would make no sense at all.

Into the cave now, the feeling familiar, then the smell. That gust of otherworldly gas, totally unlike any earthly smell. If you didn't really belong here, you would fall to the ground.

(Which, of course, was wet, pulsating—not like "ground," or "earth," or anything known here. In this world. In this solar system . . . galaxy . . . universe. . . .)

Fall to the ground, and begin hacking, your insides gurgling, the smell, the gas . . . turning you inside out.

But if you belonged here—you could take that deep breath now.

(As he did. Right now. On this last night.)

Deep. Hold it. Belonging here. One of them. Until the cave and walls gave way to . . . another place. What madmen had seen for centuries but no one ever believed was real.

They awaited him. Welcomed him.

For Betruger, he was home.

27

BY 7 A.M., DELTA LAB ALREADY SEETHED WITH activity. Well before attempting an experimental transmission, every system in Delta had to be inspected, from the power management to the dataflow integration, to the physical performance of the pods themselves.

Then there were the secondary devices, machines designed to measure and record exactly what occurred during the test. Dr. Betruger liked things checked, then rechecked, and every result brought to his attention.

Dr. Jonathan Ishii sat at his desk looking at an array of screens, each chunk of linked data flowing from one screen onto another, as power and transmission strength in the teleport pods flowed from one to the other.

Everything looked absolutely fine.

Ishii looked up. Betruger stood off to the side, with three other Delta scientists standing close by. He held his hands behind him, nodding. Like some mad general commanding an armed force all dressed in white.

How many of the others knew, Ishii wondered. How many of them *suspected?*

Ishii stole glances at the others, all so busy, whipping out PDAs, touching the holo-screens as they appeared in the air, or walking over to one of the workstations. Did any of them know . . . what really was happening here?

He saw Betruger turn and look in his direction.

Ishii reached out and touched a tab to change one of the screens to a master readout of all data being pumped into Delta's main computer system. *See,* he hoped the action said, *I'm busy, Dr. Betruger. Working hard on the project.*

Ishii kept his eyes glued to the screen now, trying to sense when Betruger took his eyes off him.

Only hours to the test. He had to go soon—and he'd have it do it in steps. Get out of here. Then he'd have to lose his sentry bot, ditch his ID tag. And slowly, without being seen, make his way out of the Delta wing, to the underground, and out—

I could die, Ishii thought.

He'd bring his PDA, of course. With all the material he had stolen from Betruger's personal files. The material that showed the truth about what was going on here. Teleportation. The ability to move across space instantly, with no real traveling at all. That was the hoax, the promise. Betruger's lie that everyone—most of them—still believed.

Ishii took a breath. *I'll stop it,* he thought. *I can do that.* And for a moment, he actually believed it.

Kane stood in an assembly room, near the marine headquarters, dressed in the standard-issue space marine fatigues—not much different from anything his division wore on Earth. A different insignia on the lapel, a belt designed to hold the PDA, key to communicating and navigating here.

Only the color of the fatigues revealed that they weren't in Kansas, or any other place that could be called Earth. Mottled a reddish orange, as if they were going to do operations on the surface of the planet.

He noticed that some of the older Marines here wore some gun-metal colored fatigues, certainly better suited to the gray environment of the interior. Maybe you had to work your way up to them.

Sergeant Kelly looked up from his PDA. "All right, newbies, you each get a section to patrol this morning. You get a four-hour cycle, then break for a twenty-minute lunch, then report back here and we'll see what else we got for you. Some of you may be reassigned to the regular units. But consider this the day that you all get—what the hell—'comfortable' with Mars City. And Christ, remember that there are a lot of civilians up here, even kids."

Kelly shook his head.

"So any of you that may have seen fighting down below, I want you to forget all that gung-ho crap. Nice steady pace, a big smile to the locals, and nothing to startle anyone. Got it?"

In unison: "Yes, Sergeant!"

"Great. And so you assholes get used to using them, I sent your teammate and assignment to your PDA. Have a great fucking morning."

Kelly turned on his heels, and Kane took out his PDA and scrolled to the flashing "Assignment" icon.

A small map appeared showing the underground area, and then a close-up of the energy processing area. Below that, his companion for the patrol.

Private Tobias Smith.

And then Smitty was there, grinning from ear to ear. Kane looked at the scrawny private. "Did you ask Kelly—"

Smitty started to deny Kane's accusation, but then looked down. "Yeah, I said we hung out. On the transport."

"Great," Kane said. And then, "Come on."

Ishii stood up. He walked to the back of Delta, over to a wall of oversized monitors that studied every inch of the lab. All linked to various sensors monitoring temperature and power demands. Ishii made a big deal of looking up, then at the readouts, when Betruger appeared at his elbow.

"All okay, Ishii?"

"Oh—fine, Dr. Betruger Just making sure my PDA link is working . . ."

"Was there a problem?"

"Er, no. Not at all. But, you know, always good to check and recheck."

For a moment Betruger didn't say anything. "Right." Another pause. "Ishii, you seem a bit nervous. Are you okay? Anything wrong?"

As soon as he started to answer, Ishii knew he was answering too quickly. "No, sir. I'm fine. Just, you know, a big test for us."

"Right, very big, Ishii. Carry on—but if you notice anything wrong"—he cleared his throat—"anything at all, you will tell me?"

"Absolutely, Dr, Betruger."

And then, like a billowing and icy fog bank, Betruger finally moved on.

"Man, that was some goddamn breakfast they gave me," Wegner said to Maria. "You ever see what they feed volunteers?"

Maria didn't answer, but Rodriguez did. "Enough food for three guys! Shit, were those real eggs?"

"They sure the hell *tasted* like real eggs. They even had yolks."

Real eggs, maybe something like real bacon, Maria thought. Exactly like the breakfast they'd give a condemned man. And this guy—Wegner—didn't see that? *Far be it from me*, Maria thought, *to tell him.*

"Hey," Rodriguez said, "that's a pretty damn cool

breakfast. And a nice package you get for doing this. Real nice. But aren't you like even a little bit worried?"

Moron, Maria thought. Kelly told them specifically to not discuss anything about the experiment. And here was Rodriguez, stirring things up.

"Nah. Figure each time it gets safer. And I haven't heard of anyone getting really hurt. Maybe they need some R and R back on Earth. But that's it, right?"

Right. And we don't hear anything about the subjects because that's how they like it.

"Guess so," Rodriguez said. "Still—"

"Rodriguez, zip it, hm? You're making my ears hurt."

He looked at her, getting a quick eye roll, and even the dense Rodriguez finally got the message. "Yeah, right, sure, Moraetes. You're the boss." The sniggering snort: *as if!*

That was another thing: There were marine escorts coming soon, assigned to accompany Wegner to Delta. And didn't that tell the giddy space marine something? Escorts, guards—to make sure he got there? The whole thing was creepy.

"Come on, Rodriguez. Lucky me—we get to patrol together today."

A few hours walking a circuit around Alpha Labs lay ahead. *Life on Mars—at its most exciting . . .*

28

ISHII WALKED SLOWLY PAST THE WALL OF MONI-
tors, looking down at his PDA as if checking that it
was synced properly. *Yes, that's what I'm doing. Just
checking things.* But he kept moving, walking close to
the main entrance of Delta. Lab assistants and scientists walked back and forth. Ishii reached the Delta
reception desk, manned by two women who, for
some strange reason, also wore lab coats.

Two burly marines stood at the main exit, and more
marines were posted at the lab's secondary exits.

Ishii walked up to the exit. Immediately a sentry
bot scurried up and took its place immediately behind him. But at his level of clearance, a sentry bot
was entirely optional.

He scrolled to a window on his PDA and, at the

security screen, hit a button to disengage the bot. It immediately scurried back to some distant corner of Reception. The marine stood perfectly still. If they suspected anything, their eyes didn't show it.

He started talking into his mouthpiece. "Yes, I'm checking on it now. Don't worry. All right. I'll make sure."

And, maintaining his stream of meaningless one-sided conversation, he slipped out into the main hall-way. One foot in front of the other, he told himself, walking away with enough data to expose everthing that had happened here and—sweet God—everything that was about to happen.

"MacDonald—where is the subject?"

Kellyn MacDonald turned away from Pod One, the delivery pod.

"He's on his way now."

Betruger nodded. "Good. I want things to go smoothly when he's here." Betruger raised his voice. "Everyone hear that? No sense of alarm, just another day in the lab—okay?"

MacDonald waited until Betruger moved away, dashing from station to station, radiating plenty of tension. Then MacDonald got up and walked back to the storage chambers in the back.

He went into one that he knew wasn't used except for discarded equipment. A bit of privacy. He began to record his special message on his PDA.

Mars City PDA
Dr. Kellyn McDonald
Personal Folder, Security Enabled.
Checked and Opened_03_13_2145 10:28:19
Sent to: Private

Recording Begun:

So, sweet Ann, it's about to happen again. Everyone knows the danger, knows what has happened. And yet—somehow—we all continue. I have told Kelliher everything, and yet, he *still* doesn't pull the plug. But this time, something worries me even more.

It's Betruger himself. Not only does he ignore the results from before. This time, he seems to be hurrying, as if we are all on some deadline. To which I might ask, deadline to what?

I don't know what will occur. I don't know what great threat the experiments may pose—to the lab, to me, to all of Mars City. I have tried to do what I can here. Now, there is nothing else for me.

Tell Patrick that I think of him tons. But please, don't say that I will see him soon. Not until we know that is a real possibility. And trust me, after this I will be doing what I can to leave this planet forever. Of course, Ann, I miss you terribly. To talk to, to be with, to be there for each other. In some ways, I've been negligent, haven't I? Perhaps like every other scientist in history, lost to their world of ideas and experiments.

I'd best end this. You never know who might come back here. But know that I think of you. And I will contact you when this hellish day is over.

Recording Ended:

Folder Closed and Locked___10:37:28

MacDonald quickly walked out of the storage room. Because of his special security clearance with Kelliher, he was able to send encrypted voice messages that Comm did not screen. They would note that he had sent a message, but that was all.

And when MacDonald rejoined his team, the test subject was already there.

"Okay," Kane said. "We turn around here."

Smitty looked down at his PDA. "You sure? It looks like—"

But Kane had already turned on his heel, completing the mindless loop he had been assigned by Kelly. Maybe doing time in some serious brig might have been better than this, he thought.

Betruger stopped and looked around the room.

He saw MacDonald walk out the rear area. *What is he doing there?*

Then he looked over at the entrance and saw his medical team talking to the subject. The man wore a broad grin.

Look how happy he is, dreaming of all the perks to come.

But something was wrong. Another look around. Where the *hell* was Ishii?

"MacDonald!" Betruger yelled. The scientist hurried over. "Have you seen Ishii?"

Betruger watched as the other scientist stopped and looked around. Ishii was gone, just as the preparations for the experiment would intensify. Another glance, seeing Ishii's station abandoned. Then Batruger thought: *Could Dr. Ishii have decoded some of the material from Site 3? Could he suspect what this is really about?* No matter. But then, where was he off to? What was he doing?

"Ishii. Any idea where he is?"

MacDonald shook his head. "No, I—"

But Betruger already had General Hayden in his ear. "General, one of my people has left Delta. I want him found and returned immediately."

Betruger didn't wait for an answer. Instead he walked over to the subject. And as he did, he forced himself to smile. Wouldn't do to alarm the man. . . .

Kane saw Kelly waiting for him at Marine Combat Prep, with a few other marines standing around.

"Kane, I have a new job for you." Kelly grinned at the others. "You like to rescue, hmm?"

Kane just kept looking at Kelly. He heard a snigger from behind. *Easy,* he told himself. "Yes, Sergeant."

"One of the white coats from Delta has gone AWOL. Left Delta apparently."

"So—aren't they free to come and go?"

Kelly grinned. "Sure they are. Whaddya think, this is a prison? Let's say . . . they're just worried about him. Sometimes the pressure, you know, gets to them, or some kind of bullshit. So I want you to go find him and bring him back."

"Does he have one of those"—Kane looked down at a security bot standing ready— "tailing him?"

"No such luck. At his level, he can override the bot. But no matter, his PDA is telling us where he's headed. So you got to follow the signal. I've had Command link your PDA to his. So—get the hell going."

"Me too, Sarge?" Smitty asked.

Kelly shook his head. "No. Don't want to make a big deal of this. So you stay here. And don't call me Sarge again, if you like staying alive. It's Sergeant." Then back to Kane: "You just go get the scientist on your own. And remember—don't hurt the bastard."

"Where is he headed?"

Kelly shook his head. "That's the weird thing, Kane. He's in the old underground wing. Leads just about nowhere—except to an abandoned EVA port and the old comm wing."

Kane looked at his PDA. And he could see that he had, along with full schematics of Mars City, a new map showing a blip tracking the scientist as he made his way underground.

Kane looked up. "Sergeant—maybe a better weapon?"

Kelly shook his head. "Nah, you got two good

USSM sidearms, with plenty of clips. And if you use them, then you will have—guess what?—fucked up again. Now move it."

There was more laughter from the marines standing around as John Kane began his solo trek to the underbelly of Mars City.

2145

THREE

THREE

2145

29

THEO LOOKED UP AT HIS MOTHER, STANDING BY some strange machine, just staring at it.

"Mom, when can we go explore?"

For a moment she didn't turn around, but then she looked back at him. "What? I was—"

"You *said* we could go exploring. I've seen everything in here. It's boring."

She smiled. Theo knew his mother wasn't too happy about coming here. Dad had told them they could have stayed on Earth. But she didn't want to do that.

At first he was glad. He was going to Mars! He was going to live on *Mars*. But so far, it didn't look so great. Sure, there were kids in Mars City. They even had some rooms where kids took lessons, like school.

And it wasn't forever. Only a year. Maybe not even that long.

"Right. I was just trying to figure out how this stove works. Too many buttons. It's so new."

Theo nodded. "Everything's new here, Mom."

"Yes, isn't it? Okay. Maybe we'll just have some cereal and then . . . I'll try to show you Mars City. They gave me this—"

She held up something small. Theo's dad had one too. Everyone seemed to have them. *Maybe I should have one too*, Theo thought. "Good. 'Cause it's small and boring in here."

Again a smile from his mother. "Maybe we can get to where your daddy works, okay? First day here, a new assignment. Could be pretty exciting."

Theo grabbed the remote. A screen flickered to life on the wall. "And where's that, Mom? Where does he work?"

"A place called Delta Labs." She turned back to the stove for one more try.

Jonathan Ishii had finally reached the old Comm Center. The few lights he saw on the console showed that the system was still linked to the energy grid. Good. That would mean he wouldn't have to trek back to Energy Processing and get power rerouted somehow.

While all the time dodging questions . . .

But was power still flowing to the outside dish? And did he understand this system well enough to get it operational? Already they would know that he was gone from the lab. Maybe they had even tracked him here. Wouldn't be long before somebody showed up.

He reached under his lab coat and grabbed the gun he had removed from storage.

He sat down at the console and, using everything he had ever learned about the data and communications systems of Mars, started bringing the abandoned Comm Center to life.

The elevator opened, and Kane was greeted by a security guard.

"Help you, Private?"

"I'm looking for someone who's gone AWOL, a Delta scientist."

The security guard shook his head. "Another one of those? The nutcases in the white coats." The guard took a few steps closer. "They're losing it left and right these days. Place is—"

Close enough that Kane could see that this guard, in his subterranean base, didn't practice much in the way of dental hygiene . . .

"—starting to get to them."

"Yeah. Did you see someone come by?"

The guard shook his head. "No. But—" He laughed, the sound echoing weirdly in the tunnel. "I can't be fucking everywhere, now can I?"

Yeah . . . people starting to lose it. And not just the scientists. "Keep your eyes open," Kane said. Not a request but, an order to the guard, who outranked him.

Then Kane headed around to the left, toward what was labeled Convergence Chamber on his PDA.

"All right, squad. You're to take positions in Alpha. The general has demanded increased security throughout the Alpha and Delta wings. That means a lot of walking, keeping your eyes open—you know the drill."

"Sergeant, got any idea why?" Rodriguez laughed at his own question. "What for?"

Maria had to wonder that too. Why today? Some big UAC VIPs here—so maybe it was all for show?

"Rodriguez, I don't think you have the clearance to even ask that question. Just hit your positions, eyes alert. Got it?"

"Yes, Sergeant."

The squad of space marines started out for Alpha. Maria wondered how Kane was doing.

"Should we go to the lab now?" Swann said.

Campbell turned to him. "I'm not going."

"But Betruger expects—"

"Screw Betruger. I want to check that the weapons shipment has all been deployed. We didn't bring that firepower up here so it could sit in metal crates for a month."

"But won't Kelliher want you to see what happens today?"

Campbell came close to Swann. "I think he wants *you* to see. And you'd best get a report out fast—good or bad. Me, he's expecting that I keep things tight as a drum up here. If we shut Betruger down, it won't be pretty."

"You won't need weapons." Swann made a small nervous laugh. "I mean, just to shut down a lab."

"Hey, counselor—it's Mars. Anything can happen."

Campbell started for the Combat Prep room, leaving Swann alone to head to Delta.

"All right, Private. Just stay still."

Wegner looked at the medical doctor who plunged a syringe into his bicep. A tube ran from the syringe into a vial. Wegner watched as one vial filled with his blood. The doctor removed that vial, then placed another vial at the end of the tube.

After four vials, Wegner joked, "Hey, Doc, leave some for me, okay?"

The doctor turned to him, not a bit of a smile on his pinched face. "We need these samples for before and after. To monitor any changes."

Wegner laughed. "The only change I want to monitor is my getting out of here."

Though he stood naked as people walked back and forth, he didn't feel self-conscious at all. Giving some of them a thrill, he thought.

They had explained to Wegner that he had to enter the chamber without any clothes. And in moments, he'd appear in the other chamber. Just like magic.

The boss scientist, a squat man with a massive head, walked up. "Is the subject ready?"

The doctor taking blood turned around, quick to respond. *He barks, and they jump. Just like the freakin' military.* "Yes, Dr. Betruger."

Then the one called Betruger turned to someone at his elbow, trailing close behind him. "MacDonald, prepare the pod chambers. All Delta science teams to their stations. We begin exactly at noon."

Another man in a white coat came and took Wegner's arm and began leading him to one of the large nearby chambers. The stone floor felt cold under his bare feet.

Betruger watched the lab in motion, everyone hurrying now. Like ants, scurrying, racing around, all imagining that this was really another experiment.

Ah, the things they didn't know. The things that they would soon realize.

Though there was this one concern: Ishii. What had his data chief seen? What had he been able to figure out? Whatever he tried to tell them, they would probably write off Dr. Ishii as only another nut, someone else who has mysteriously gone mad in Mars City.

Did the scientist really expect to escape, leave, or—

Betruger's eyes darted right and left, looking at the

swirl of activity in Delta, but as if trying to look inside his own head, into his mind filled with secrets.

What could Ishii be doing? What could he know?

Betruger didn't like not having the answers. But soon none of it would matter.

He turned to Pod One. One of the assistants had opened the door while the medical supervisor, the mealy-mouthed Leprine, carefully guided the subject into the pod. The man grinned as people watched him enter, then walk to the center of the pod. Betruger looked around. He had invited Swann to come. Less an invitation, and more of an order.

Betruger touched his earpiece. "Hayden," he said quietly.

Then after the chirp of a signal, he heard the general's voice. "What is it?"

"Where is Swann? He should be here."

"He should be there any minute, Doctor."

Betruger hit his earpiece again, killing the connection. Then, standing there, he whispered, so low that even someone standing next to him wouldn't hear what sounded like words . . .

(Though they would see the lips move, slowly, as if mumbling.)

"Astaroth ag-ignome . . . pendar . . . my'el R'yleh . . ."

Repeating the words, the sounds, over and over—inaudible, he knew, except to those for whom they were intended.

30

THEO'S MOTHER SAT DOWN FACING HIM. "THERE," she said smiling. "I figured out how to work it. Some nice hot cereal."

Theo looked down at the bowl. Little clouds of steam rose from the bowl.

He looked back at his mother. "What is this stuff?"

She shrugged. "Hot cereal. Just like we have back home . . ." Then she hurried to add words. "On Earth."

Another look down at the bowl. "It doesn't look like the cereal on Earth." A deep sniff. "Or smell like it."

His mom rolled her eyes. "Just eat it, Theo, okay?"

"And then we can explore?"

"Yes—and then you and me . . . explore this place."

• • •

The panels in front of Dr. Ishii came alive. One large screen showed that now he had a direct signal to the large dish outside.

But that didn't mean that a message here would get out.

Ishii looked at the clock above the control board. How much time did he have to do this?

And then—

(*Oh God, oh God, oh God . . .*)

Would they believe him? A screen to his right changed. Words.

"DST Activated and Ready."

The old Comm Center was online, separate from the main controls of Mars City. Ready for deep space transmission.

Ishii reached for the controls.

Kane moved quickly. Something about this place down here made him feel that time might be of the essence. Not just a crap mission Kelly dumped on him. Something to remind Kane of his status here. And with that, a feeling that he best be careful.

He was tempted to break into a jog, curving around the massive Convergence Chamber, when someone stepped out of the shadows.

"Hey, marine—where the hell *you* goin'? Nothing down here."

Kane stopped. The man's nameplate said "C. Rodgers."

"You see someone come by here?" Kane said.

"Me, no. Just got here. They like this thing checked every eight hours. Always the same. Don't know why we check it."

The guy sounded spaced. Could they get drugs down here, stuff to drink? Why not—you could probably get it anywhere.

Kane took a step closer to the man. "One of the scientists. He could have come this way. See anyone?"

Rodgers shook his head. "Just you." Rodgers laughed. "And to be honest . . . I'm not even seeing you too well."

Kane started moving again.

"What are we supposed to do here?" Rodriguez said.

Maria looked at him. "Look like you're guarding something."

Rodriguez looked around Alpha Lab. "Man, this place is big. What the hell they do here?"

Maria ignored the question. But she had to admit, this was strange, all the marine squads now posted throughout Mars City.

She looked at her PDA, wishing she'd been paired up with someone else, *anyone* else.

Campbell made sure the door to the weapons room just off Combat Prep was closed tight and locked behind him. He went to the gleaming silver crate. Unlike the other crates that had arrived in the transport, this one featured an electronic lock. No one was getting a look inside the crate, past the reinforced titanium shell, without the code.

Campbell entered a series of six numbers. The red readout changed to green, and he heard a series of loud metallic clicks.

He waited, then started to open the crate, undoing the latches that girded the top of the crate. Not an easy task. It took his full strength.

And there, inside, the prize. The secret.

Up, up, until the crate was fully open. A second case lay beneath, but this one was constructed of molded plastic compound designed to cushion what was inside.

He popped two latches and opened that.

And there it was. What the weapons team back at UAC dubbed the BFG. Almost too much gun for one person to hold, even someone with the upper-body strength of Campbell.

He was tempted to take it out, but someone without clearance could walk in here.

It was, quite simply, a thing of beauty. Enough firepower so that one person could hold back a small army. Campbell shut the plastic cover, then slowly, carefully, the metallic crate top, which automatically locked.

A small army.

Who knows, he thought. *Stranger things have happened.*

·   ·   ·

Swann walked into the lab. The volunteer stood naked in one of the pods, his eyes watching the scientists moving around.

Betruger looked over at Swann, but then went back to talking to his scientific team, moving between monitors and control panels. *Maybe I cut it a little close*, Swann thought.

He looked at a massive digital clock, counting down to the thousandth of a second. Just about five minutes to go, assuming they stuck to the exact timetable for the experiment.

31

THEO FOLLOWED BESIDE HIS MOTHER, HOLDING her hand. She had led him back to where the spaceship first had landed, but then she took him down a new hallway.

It wasn't that much fun at all.

"Where we going?" he finally asked.

"Mars City is big. Can't see it all in one shot, Theo. But I thought I'd show you where the soldiers stay, the space marines."

"Why are they called 'space' marines?"

He heard his mother laugh. "Because we're in space." But then the laugh stopped, and her voice sounded different. "I mean, I guess that's why."

Ishii entered the coordinates of the communication target. He had thought to send the message directly to Earth, but who knew what filters the UAC satellite grid used. Could be the message would simply die in space.

But the armada . . .

They would get everything as they patrolled the space lanes between Mars and Earth.

It took a few moments for the target coordinates to lock. Ishii waited.

And then there was a voice behind him and a hand on his shoulder.

Lost in getting the system up and running, the scientist hadn't even heard Kane walk into the old Comm Center.

As soon as Kane got there, he heard a voice in his ear. "Kane—Kelly here. Find that damn scientist and get your ass back here." A snicker. "Unless you need reinforcements."

Kane didn't acknowledge Kelly's barking command.

"Doctor . . . Dr. Ishii, please step away from the console."

The scientist turned. Then Kane could see his eyes, wide, bloodshot, like a grunt who'd been in battle for days, no sleep, no food. *War eyes,* they called them—acquired by humans in battle who begin mutating into killing machines, with only one thought: kill the other guy and keep me the hell alive.

Ishii spoke. "No. You don't understand. I—I have to do this."

Kane took another step closer to him. "Doctor, I've been ordered to stop you doing . . . whatever you're doing, and bring you back."

Ishii nodded. "Of course. That's what they would want. But—" The rheumy bloodshot eyes looked up at him. "You have to understand, you see, I know. I *know* what they're going to do."

What the hell is he talking about? Kane wondered. So far, Mars City seemed more like an extension of the mental ward back at the new VA, in the hills of Colorado.

He watched Ishii begin to move close to some switches near the side of the console. A microphone—kind of primitive—veered from the center of the control board. *He's about to send a message. How bad could that be?*

But Kane couldn't risk getting into any more trouble. *I just want to stay under the damn radar . . .*

Ishii's fingers moved slowly, as if by stealthily making their way to the "Transmit" buttons, he wouldn't be seen.

Kane had no choice. He moved quickly to Ishii, his hands closing on the scientist's wrist. "Step away, Doctor. Just step . . . away . . . from the console."

Ishii turned, and up close, Kane could see the fear in the probably mad scientist's eyes. *This whole place is a loony bin,* Kane thought.

"No. You don't understand. You have to let me—" Ishii still tried to hit some buttons with his free hand. But Kane moved quickly, imprisoning that hand too, and then, just so the scientist got the message, whipping him back, pulling him and the chair back against the wall.

And then—an amazing moment as Kane spun around. He could see . . . this room, this old Communications Center suddenly had a panoramic window looking out on Mars. There was no Mars City out there, nothing but the reddish ridges, the mountainous areas, burning in the midday sun. A temperature readout by the window told the current temperature: 271 degrees Kelvin.

For the first time an awareness of where he was hit Kane.

But then Ishii struggled against his grip. "Listen, er—" The man's wild eyes searched Kane's uniform. "Private Kane, you *have* to listen to me!"

"Sure. Then you are coming back with me. Understand?"

The man nodded. Kane released his grip.

"This place . . . what's going on here . . . it's not what they tell you." He laughed. "It's not what they tell *anyone*. Even the scientists in the lab, even they don't know. But I do." His voice rose. "I do."

Right, thought Kane. *Funny thing about delusions.*

"And what is that, Dr. Ishii?"

"You're not going to believe me."

Good chance of that . . . "We won't know until we try."

Ishii looked away, looked at the open landscape, as if the answer lay somewhere out there. "It happened hundreds of thousands of years ago, maybe millions. It happened right here. And God, sweet God in heaven, it's going to happen again."

"Excuse me, ma'am, but I'm afraid your clearance doesn't let you go any further."

Theo held his mother's hand tight. The soldier stood in the center of the hallway. He looked big, so much bigger than his father, wearing all sorts of padding. He held a rifle of some kind, something really cool. None of Theo's army guys had any weapons like that.

He'd have to ask his dad what it was, next time he saw him.

His mother smiled down at him.

"We're new. Just giving my son a little tour. Show him some more of Mars City. This"—she touched a badge on her lapel—"doesn't let us go down here?"

Theo felt the soldier's eyes drift down. "No, ma'am. This is a military wing of the city, and you would need military clearance."

She nodded. Then she turned to Theo.

"Sorry, Theo. Maybe Daddy can arrange something for us. I'll talk to him when he gets back tonight."

Theo wasn't sure he wanted to go down this way anyway. It didn't look very interesting. He felt his mom give him a tug, pulling him away. But then—

"Miss, I can't let you go down there, not alone. But if you want to give the boy a quick look, he can catch a glimpse of where the marines line up before getting assigned, where we get our gear." The big soldier smiled. *He seems to like Mom*, Theo thought. "I'll just walk you down there a bit."

The soldier smiled down at Theo. And though he didn't really want to walk down there, he and his mom followed the marine.

Elliot Swann stood by the lab entrance. After watching this experiment, he had a lot of reports to go through. Every aspect of Mars City had to be signed off on by Kelliher—and it was Swann's job to make sure nothing was missed.

Only another minute or so.

The naked subject in the pod was grinning. Every scientist seemed to have something to do, something to keep their eyes off him.

Maybe, Swann thought, *I'm the only person really looking at him. Hope it goes well, you stupid bastard. Just don't be like the others. Guess he never heard the adage— never volunteer.*

Two minutes left. A message on his PDA, from Campbell. "How'd it go?"

Too soon. Swann was about to respond, but then decided to simply wait. In a few minutes he'd have something to send back. Then he could get on with his work.

Rodriguez looked down one of the long empty tunnels of Alpha.

"You think Hayden ordered all this security?"

Maria shook her head. She guessed it had something to do with today's visitors. She pulled her weapon close, and without even being aware of it at first, tightened her finger around the trigger.

"I'm listening," said Kane.

Ishii nodded. "What Betruger is doing in there . . . has nothing to do with teleportation. Not anymore, at least. Not since he discovered what it does, what those machines can do here."

"Which is?"

Ishii seemed annoyed at the question. "They don't *move* things from one place to another. Not really. No one who has been a test subject has been able to say what happened to them. Not even the ones who came back still looking . . . human."

Kane shifted on his feet. This guy was one for the books.

"Betruger knew—he *knew*—they went somewhere, that by using those pods, he opened a way into those places, that you could—"

Okay, thought Kane, *enough of this*. In seconds Kelly would be in his ear again, bellowing for him to double-time it back with the scientist. "Sir, we really—"

"He didn't know that I saw everything from Site 3, what he had learned. About what happened so many years ago here. He *knows* what that thing is— the artifact—what he called the Soul Cube. All those living beings long ago, their need to stop it, their terrible sacrifice—"

"Look, Doctor—you're losing me, and we have to get back, we got to leave—"

Ishii backed up against the panoramic glass window. Kane had no choice but to go grab him and start dragging the man back. But then in his earpiece, he heard a sharp burst of something like static.

High-pitched, as if some radio signal was being stretched and pulled and distorted into an ear-piercing level of volume.

Kane yanked the earpiece out.

Then—

It was almost like standing before an open window. *A breeze coming through a window on a summer's day.* Turning, now stronger. The breeze, now the wind of a storm. The steady sound of wind rushing during a summer storm on Earth. Growing. Now a roar.

Kane stood there and felt the amazing blast of what had to be a racing jet of air smashing into the enclosed space of the room.

32

WITH INSTINCTS BORN OF COUNTLESS FIREFIGHTS, dodging bullets, grenades and bombs exploding all around, Kane spun to his right to what, somehow, he had registered as cover. He curled up as tight as possible, head tucked under, arms and hands tucked tight into the body.

The roaring locomotive of air blasted into the room as if it would blow the walls out, and the Martian heat would cook him and Ishii in a matter of moments.

He didn't look up. But then he heard another noise, a shrill scream, nearly an animal sound. Maybe caused by the sudden vacuum created by the air bellows?

That was followed by an ear-piercing hissing noise, static raised to an unbearable volume, intolerable heights of pitch. Kane quickly covered his ears with his hands. In the motion, his eyes closed.

But they picked up something else now blasting into the room.

A light—deep red, brilliant, the intensity of the sun in the room. He thought, *It's like the world is on fire . . .*

For a moment Kane felt something pulling at his flesh, this new light, this heat, this brilliant red glow somehow tugging on his skin.

But Kane—still protected—hugged closer to the metal barrier that led back to the Convergence Chamber. Behind his tightly closed eyes, he could see the light fade. Then—of course—came the new sound.

The sound that trailed in the wake of this red tide of light.

And as this new screaming, roaring noise cut so easily through the covering made by his hands pressed tight, Kane noticed his hands shaking.

His knees tucked close, shaking also.

And he knew that in all the battles he'd been in, in all the times he had faced death, it never, ever, felt quite as bad as this.

Maria looked at Rodriguez, his goofy mouth open, looking down the hallway. Her hair blew off her forehead, her cheek.

She thought of something then: funny thing—the breeze a fist made as it sailed close by your face, close enough to generate that little wind, and then goes flying safely by . . . a miss.

A miss. Because you ducked. You weaved. You bobbed. The thought clarified.

You moved.

And she saw an alcove leading to an Alpha Lab storage area. Narrow, dark, but away from this now growing roar of wind, this roar clearing the way for something else to come.

Theo let his mother's hand go. Maybe it was the funny wind.

The soldier had stopped. He started to turn. His mother stood there. Her hand reached out, looking for Theo's hand.

Theo went to grab that hand, latch on, hold on, hold it tight—

When whatever came into the tunnel threw Theo back. Pushed him back hard, then smacked him down onto the floor. He screamed. He did what every kid does. He called for his mother.

"Mom! Mommy!"

But still this wind kept pushing him, like a playground bully, pushing, sweeping him away, until Theo felt himself fly up as if he was paper, now thrown against a wall, then down another corridor.

And then there was nothing.

Swann flew back against the door.

Both pods now glowed an incredible red, like

massive flames erupting from the floor. Did the pods even still exist? Each one shot out jagged spears of reddish lights, in every direction, penetrating the walls of the lab, shooting every which way.

In that moment Swann knew he was alive because of where he stood. And as long as one of those spears didn't hit him, those sharp points of fiery red light shooting all over, then he was fine.

He laughed. A weird feeling.

When so many fell around him, tumbling to the ground, the light skewering right through them. Scientists who only seconds ago were walking around checking everything, now lay writhing on the ground.

Because—and this was the sick thing—those spears rocketing out of the twin pods, when they hit something alive—they didn't just move through them. No, like hooking a human worm, they jabbed into the person on the floor, legs kicking, head arching up and then smacking down to the floor. Toying. Playing.

Swann shook his head. *No. Not playing with them. Doing something else.*

He turned right. One person stood nearby, unaffected as the rolling spears flew into and out of the lab. Betruger. Standing there. His skin seemed red, then, for a second, rippling. He held something in his hands. Like a shield, filled with curves and protrusions.

What the hell is that?

Until finally Swann looked at the pod to the right.

Where the volunteer had been standing only seconds ago, smiling, all thumbs-up and okay.

He was still there. Sort of. Only now what had once been his naked chest was this gaping hole. A hole that seemed to pulse and grow larger as the spears shot out. And out of that hole, things came out.

Swann looked at one. Something with a head, a big smiley face of teeth, and snakelike legs somehow helping it move.

He looked away.

Because more things came out, different things, things that Swann didn't want to see. He knew he was shaking, heaving and crying as he stood there, somehow miraculously alive.

But another glance at the fireworks explosion that was Delta Lab . . .

Scientists, once speared, shot through with the electric red bolts, now . . . yes . . . standing up, slowly getting to their feet, slowly, studiously. (This was new to them, after all.) They were *alive.*

But then one of them nearby turned to Swann, and he knew that wasn't quite right. Not alive in the way they were only seconds ago.

The nearby one, whose loopy jaw now seemed to be able to open double-wide, tilted its head, seeing Swann.

Noticing him. Swann's right hand felt the edge of the open lab exit.

He turned, not even able to worry that there might be something there, right there outside, waiting for him to spin around and turn and try to get out of the lab.

And Swann started running as fast as he could, unaware that as he ran, his screams resounded throughout the corridor.

33

AND SO IT WAS DONE. MALCOLM BETRUGER heard the chittering as they emerged, crawling out of the hole that simply grew wider.

It was all so *wonderful*. A life spent trying to create miracles, and he never dreamed that there was this. This other reality, waiting for someone to just wedge that door open a bit.

As the beings crawled out, they ignored him, like newborn babies, oblivious of their parents. No matter. Betruger could hear the voices in his head all the time. Much of it was incomprehensible, of course. There was so much to learn! But at other times quite clear, telling him to watch the pods, observe as the opening grew larger. He knew it wasn't just happening here either.

No. Now the planet itself seethed with the power and energy flowing into it. This was simply like a radio receiver, channeling those waves of energy, letting things move from there to here, following the commands as they—

Betruger took a breath.

—as they reclaimed this planet. And it was all only the beginning.

He looked down at his arms. The skin rippled as if waves moved just under the surface, making the skin first bulge a bit, then turn smooth.

Then—what he held in his hands. Almost a gift.

I am ready, Betruger thought, *for whatever they wish to do with me.*

The lights flickered out in the service tunnel, then— perhaps fed by the emergency backup—they flickered on at what looked like half power.

Sergeant Kelly scrambled to his feet. He looked around at the other marines that had been standing near him, in this corridor away from the large reactor room of Delta.

"Come on, get up! Get the hell up."

No one moved, so he gave a quick kick to the boots of one of the jarheads. A groan. Though . . . there was something about the sound.

"Come on. We have to secure this goddamn—"

The marine turned. At first all Kelly could do was look at the private's hands. Blackened things, as if they had reached into some blisteringly hot oven and yanked out a burning log, fingers curled tightly around it.

But then the face tilted back. Except it wasn't a face, this thing making a low grunting sound. In place of a human face was a distorted and twisted near-clown image. The mouth slit sideways, as if someone had taken a knife and slashed it to make it open wider. And eyes, vacant dull back pits in yellowish goo.

The hair—what was left of it—had turned white and stringy.

The space marine made another low barking, grunting sound, and started to get up.

Kelly instinctively backed away.

Just as the other two marines also started to move, both in the same condition.

Kelly raised his gun. He was about to say something but he hesitated because—sweet Jesus—it sure looked as though they wouldn't be able to understand a word he said.

Kane looked around the room. Signs of the shockwave, or whatever had hit the room, dotted the walls and the floor.

But otherwise, everything appeared normal.

Ishii still stood, facing out to the Martian landscape.

Whatever the hell happened, Kane felt he'd best get this runaway scientist back, and then find out what had just happened to make his first full day in Mars City so memorable.

"Doctor, we have to go."

Ishii started to turn slowly. For a moment Kane didn't notice anything out of order. The man was backlit by the still-bright Martian midday sun. But when Ishii leaped—*leaped*—at Kane, he could see that the scientist was *gone*, replaced by something that now, apparently, wanted to latch onto Kane.

The doctor's mouth was open, hands extended.

Kane dodged, but Ishii, moving amazingly quickly now, spun around and with his open jaw, snapped sharply at Kane's leg. Kane moved his leg out of reach of the man's snapping mouth. He heard the sick *click* as teeth locked together.

Now Ishii, on all fours, tried to scurry toward Kane even as the marine backed away, farther into the shadows of the old Comm Center.

He got a good look at the man's eyes, and he knew one thing: Ishii was gone, and if this thing was allowed to get a grip on him, it would all end very badly.

He tried some gentle persuasion at first, removing one of his pistols and smacking at the scientist's head as he tried to crab-claw toward Kane.

The blow made a loud thud and sent the creature rolling to the side. But again—so fast—it popped up, jumping to a standing position, mouth agape. Teeth so clear, and beyond . . . the tongue . . . a ragged piece of reddish meat, protruding, tasting the air like a snake.

Ishii pulled back for another leap.

Right onto me, Kane thought. *And what, a bite onto my neck, and what then—do I die, or become like him?*

Ishii started his leap.

Kane fired. Bullets ripped into Ishii's chest, and the man fell at Kane's feet. Then, amazingly, it looked up, started to get up again despite just having taken three rounds of high-powered projectiles to its midsection.

Guess bullets there don't do any good, Kane thought. *Live and learn.*

There was nowhere else for him to retreat. The scientist's eyes looked hungry, eager, sensing that Kane was cornered.

There was a line somewhere, an old play from school, maybe some book—something about eyes being the window to the soul. If that was the case, this thing had no soul.

But those same eyes told Kane what to do.

He blasted the thing square in the head with four rounds. Craterlike holes opened up in the skull, but still it moved, only now those blackened hands reaching for its head as if trying to repair the damage.

Still goddamn moving . . .

More blasts, until there really wasn't much of skull there at all, like some kind of humanoid vegetable where the top has been roughly bitten off, leaving only a lifeless trunk.

Until—finally—that trunk fell forward, immobile.

And Kane had a key bit of information. These things could in fact be killed.

Ishii's PDA lay on the floor. *Don't think he'll be needing that*, Kane thought as he picked it up.

He put his radio back in his ear. It was time to get moving.

Welcome to Mars City, indeed.

34

THE EARPIECE SQUAWKED TO LIFE AGAIN. AN-other screech, a burst of static, then a voice . . .

A human voice. And as Kane moved through the underground corridors, he was glad to hear it.

"Kane? Kane, you down there?"

"Yes, Sergeant. I'm down here."

Kane kept up his pace, rounding the curve of the Convergence Chamber. A blast of gunfire, yells in his ear that drowned out Kelly's voice.

"Try that again, Sergeant."

"The condition, damn it. What's your—"

More gunfire. Kane knew that Kelly was near Delta, an area that Kane hadn't seen on the grand tour. And things didn't sound good . . .

"I'm alive. Not too sure about anyone else down there. Not—"

He came out to the intersection leading to the elevator out of this maze. He saw the worker who had greeted him earlier.

One arm looked blown away, replaced by a tweedy stump. An eye dangled out of its socket, hanging by threads. Enough to kill any human.

And like Ishii, he now started moving to attack, its jaws chomping at the air as if getting ready to chow down on a nice juicy steak.

Kane stopped. "Fuck . . ."

Now, both guns out, he began blasting. By instinct, he targeted the heart, but when that didn't slow the worker, he raised both guns, their arcs nearly convergent, aimed at the maintenance worker's head.

"Kane, what's happening?"

More blasts in his ear from Kelly's position.

Then: "Kane—Maria here. You okay?"

Maria. In Alpha.

"Just a minute—"

He pulled both triggers, and the automatic handguns started drilling the worker's head. Until there wasn't a head anymore.

Yeah, thought Kane, some jail time in the states might have been the better option.

He turned back to the elevator door, which was when he saw some other grunts had just arrived— three marines just ahead. For a split second, Kane didn't feel alone.

•   •   •

Maria heard Kane's gun blasts. She was about to check if he was okay, when things got a bit too busy for her in Alpha.

The thing that used to be Rodriguez lay at her feet, dead, its body riddled with shells from her weapon.

Andy Kim and Deuce Howard, both also in Bravo Company, and both amazingly okay, came running up to her.

"What the hell happened to Rodriguez?" Kim yelled. "Did you—"

Maria nodded. "Listen, Kelly is in and out. And who the hell knows where Hayden is. I think we better try to secure this area."

Deuce Howard laughed. "You mean 'secure,' like make sure if anyone else goes Rodriguez's route they also get killed?"

"Yeah. That's exactly what I mean."

Kim gave Maria's shoulder a bump. "So you're the boss lady now?"

"We could debate strategy, if you like, while these things start spreading throughout the city. And speaking of that, how the hell did you two miss that blast?"

Kim grinned. "We sneaked off into a storage room for a smoke. We have spots where the air detectors are off. A little technique we developed. Though I think the whole computer system is all screwed up."

"I bet," she said. "Okay, let's hit the corridors together. Eyes open. Not sure what happens if one of those things—"

"You mean the zombies?"

They both turned to Howard.

"Zombies?"

He nodded. "What the hell else you gonna call 'em?"

"Zombies . . ." Maria repeated.

The three of them started running down the half-lit corridors of Alpha.

Jack Campbell stood up in the weapons room. The lights had gone out, and for a few moments after the blast—

An earthquake? A reactor explosion?

—he was knocked to the floor in total darkness. After the lights flickered back on, he felt the back of his head. A gash, some blood.

But he wasted no time going to his PDA, scrolling down to Swann's ID. For a few seconds there was no signal. The shockwave must have taken down the communications system throughout the city.

He touched the contact icon again and this time heard the chirp of the signal connecting. Then a voice: "Y-yes."

About as frightened a single word as Campbell ever heard.

"Hey," Kane called, "you guys know—"

The trio turned slowly, in a way that was already

becoming sickeningly familiar. They used to be space marines.

Used to be, Kane thought.

Now, who knew what the hell they were. They started moving toward him, faster than Ishii.

All that good marine training, Kane guessed. Semper fi'.

He whipped out his handguns, while they prepared to level a range of much meatier weapons at him. Kane's eyes darted left and right, looking for cover.

He spotted a niche backing up to what looked like a storage locker, and he quickly moved into it.

Great. This is just perfect. Boxed in here, while they keep coming.

Bullets from their weapons, the machine guns, and blasts from their high-powered rapid-fire shotguns, started pinging and ricocheting and blasting into the walls beside Kane.

No. This would never do.

He crouched down, and when there was the slightest letup in the hail of bullets, he leaned out, crouched as low as possible.

It took only seconds for the three marines to see that Kane had gone down to the ground. In that moment Kane fired straight up, wasting no time on body shots, instead blasting away at the skulls. Shots immediately sent two of their skullcaps flying to the ceiling, while the entire corner was sprayed with their blood.

But even in the dim light, Kane could see that their blood wasn't red anymore.

Was it even blood? Or something else?

The two marines, now largely headless, stumbled back, then down to the ground, knees smacking hard to the ground.

But where was number three?

The answer came suddenly, surprisingly, from the side as something curled around Kane's neck, tightened, and with amazing strength yanked him to his feet.

Maria worked with Kim and Deuce, forming a three-person phalanx. Some of the zombies—

(She had now accepted that term. After all, what other word could they use?)

—were workers. And they moved slowly, stupidly. Without any weapons, they were easily dispatched.

Maria recognized some of the distorted faces, men, women she had seen in the corridors of Mars City, or in the cafeteria. Now twisted, misshapen, like wax faces left out in the hot midday sun.

"Christ," said Deuce. "This is too much. What the hell—"

"Easy," said Kim. "We got other company."

Maria glanced back at Kim's corner of their three-point defensive position. Space marines coming toward them, now zombies, dragging their weapons like kids might drag a teddy bear.

But then, one—a guy Maria had seen for a year

and hadn't said more than two words to—started to pull up and aim his dragged weapon.

"Hell, they're going to fire at us!" she said. "Kim, keep those others away. I'm going to turn."

Then she spun around so that now both she and Deuce faced the marines. She fell to one knee and raised her machine gun, sending an arc of fire flying right up one zombie marine's body as if trying to create perforation lines right up the center.

But then that creature kept coming and started to raise his weapon.

"Damn," she heard Deuce say. She felt Kim at her back, plugging away at the civilians.

Then she looked at the zombie's poached-egg eyes, the dime-sized pupils moving back and forth.

Fucker's trying to take aim. Let's see how he does that without eyes.

Maria blasted both sockets. And not only did it stop the zombie from taking a shot, but she had stopped it cold.

"Good, I got one—"

But then next to her she heard a groan. Deuce dropped his weapon, and his hands went to his chest where an opening bloomed, squirting blood.

Maria only glanced at her dead partner, then returned to shoot at the zombie about to attempt to blow her away.

"Bastard," she said, firing. "Eat this—"

And she sent a half-dozen shots neatly into the thing's head.

"Maria, Deuce, I got them, I think—"

Andy Kim turned around and saw Deuce on the ground, the open chest wound still gurgling.

Deuce Howard's lifeless eyes were beyond caring.

"Come on," Maria said. "We got to clear this area. God knows how many more of these are walking around."

Kim seemed frozen, numb, glued to the ground.

"Come on Andy. He's gone! Now get the hell up."

And finally Kim stood up and they started walking through the corridors of Alpha.

"All right, listen up, Swann. Are you someplace safe?"

Campbell waited.

"I—I think so. Quiet here. Nothing coming out of Delta. Doors sealed, I think."

"Good. That's good. Okay, here's what we're going to do . . ."

Campbell imagined Swann crouched in some dark corner, shivering maybe, his body a wreck from fear.

Got to give him a little steel, Campbell thought. *Get some balls into the guy.*

"You've done good, Swann. You're out of the lab. You're alive, safe. I'm going to try to secure Administration, get Hayden to make sure that this part of Mars City is clear."

"Right."

"But I need you—"

He heard a breath of air.

"*We* need you to get to the Comm Center. It's the only way to get a communication out to deep space until all systems are back up and running. We're going to need reinforcements. The armada is out there, just circling. Describe the situation—"

"The situation? The situation! Campbell, what the hell is—"

"Swann. Calm down. You hear me?" He raised his voice. "Okay. I don't know what it is, counselor. But whatever the hell is going on here, we can't handle it ourselves. So, someone has to get that message out, someone with the clearance to have it listened to. You're over there; it has to be you."

Nothing for a second.

"Swann, you still there?"

"Yes."

"Can you do this?"

A longer wait. Definitely a lot to put on the plate of the UAC's legal mouthpiece.

"I can do it."

"Good. Stick to the shadows, watch every step. But move fast."

"Okay."

"Let me know when you get there."

"Okay."

"Oh, and Swann? Good luck."

"Right."

The signal went dead.

Good luck—because the poor bastard was going to need it. *In fact, we all are.*

He looked down at the massive chunk of firepower that was the BFG.

Campbell touched it.

You and me, hm? My new best friend.

Just in case it all goes south here . . .

35

THEO LEANED OUT TO LOOK BACK AT THE HALL-way, back to his mother and the nice soldier who had been with them.

The soldier was *gone,* and his mother stood there, her back to him.

Maybe, Theo thought, *she's looking for me. Can't find me. She's probably scared, worried; she always worries so much.*

He crawled out a bit more from his hiding place.

"Mom?" he said. Then louder, "Mommy?"

And now she turned.

Slowly . . .

And in that slow movement Theo felt something was wrong. Something must have happened to his mom during that explosion. She was moving *so* slowly.

Until she turned and faced him. What had been her blouse was ripped in places. And he saw blood.

For a second, Theo felt worried about his mom. She had been hurt.

But that was before he looked up to her face.

Her eyes.

He remembered . . .

Their last week on Earth. Walking past a house. Toys in the yard, a plastic riding car, some soft darts, and there was this clown-head toy.

Not smiling. Almost looking mean, mad—and on top of its head, a hat, like an upside-down ice cream cone. With a hole on top—and you could shove things into the clown's head.

Theo had looked at it as he walked past the house. The face, so scary. Thinking: maybe you could stuff things in the head and make the clown smile.

And now—

His mother's face—

(Thinking, *It's not my mommy's face. That's not her, that's not her, that's not her—!*)

He screamed as she walked to him, like a baby learning to walk, but then a bit faster. Her eyes all bulgy like melted marshmallows, the mouth sliding around, opening, shutting, maybe trying to speak.

He kept screaming, and now his mother was only steps away, and Theo couldn't even move.

Kane dangled off the floor, held up by this huge chunk of muscle, gristle-like, tightening, closing his windpipe. Then the soldier holding him up started shaking Kane left and right, dragging him across the floor.

In seconds it would all be over.

If he didn't get some damn oxygen into him in seconds, then this day on Mars was over.

His left hand still held a gun. But that arm was pinned by the two-armed grip of the twisted marine that held him.

But that hand still had a gun. He felt that the thing's grip was weaker on his other arm. He might be able to work that arm free—

In those precious seconds . . .

He tried to stretch his right hand over and close on the gun stock, but he could barely graze the muzzle. A bit more grunting stretch, even as he felt that the thing might try ripping Kane's neck in half, its forearm mutated into a constrictor-like coil.

His fingers closed on the muzzle. His left hand let go. And now, holding the muzzle as tight as he could, he tensed, and then he used all his right arm strength to break that arm free.

Nothing happened.

Another grunt. And then the sweat, and some sticky slime oozing from the marine's skin must have made it a bit more slippery, and his right arm was *free*.

At the same time his right foot touched the ground.

He had to move fast. An option that he hoped that thing holding him didn't have.

Kane now had to shift the hold on the handgun by making his fingers crab-crawl over its surface, turning the muzzle to face out, then grabbing the handle.

Then, with the thing about to reapply its death grip, he brought the freed arm up.

The gun muzzle jabbed instantaneously under the chin of the thing, and then three quick blasts.

It took a second for the marine's body to react.

But then Kane's two feet were once again on the ground, the viselike grip released and, like a boa uncurling, the flesh noose around his neck unwound.

The thing tumbled back. Kane noticed that he had been sprayed with whatever came out of the thing's head—a sick slimy purple.

He hurried to the elevator, and the way back up.

MacDonald held his arms tight across his chest, as if holding his arms that way might somehow make him safe.

Not that the things coming into the lab, the creatures now pouring out of the ever widening opening that used to be Pod One showed any interest in him at all. He noticed that a few tall things, nearly human-looking with legs and heads, would take a few steps and . . .

Disappear. But to where?

He noticed that he mumbled, sitting there, curled tight. Talking to himself as a lifeline to sanity.

Got to keep talking to myself, he thought.

Simple words and phrase—*No, what's that, have to watch, have to tell people, have to, have to—*

Betruger, carrying something, had vanished into the pulsating opening, now glowing with a dozen shades of fiery crimson.

(Into it!)

MacDonald looked down at his PDA.

But the screen said very calmly, very matter-of-factly, "Local failure: all communication links currently disabled."

So for now, there was no one to tell, and nothing to do but sit and watch.

First the walls glowed, the network of circuitlike spirals and connections suddenly . . . now on.

And Axelle became momentarily distracted from the fact that she couldn't see a way out of this subterranean trap back to the surface. Only a few air tanks lay cached down here.

And after that?

But then the colors began changing, the walls pulsing with color. She heard a low rumbling sound.

(Sounds from below. Deeper into this hole . . .)

What's happening? What is this? she asked herself. But nothing in her work on Earth or Mars came even close to suggesting an answer.

Then—a horrible moment—she felt the ground below her *move*. Initially the ground rumbled a bit, the red dirt and rocks that sealed whatever this tunnel was, began to shift. The rocky cover, the cap to the tunnel, broke up into shards as if mere ice floes, and all this heat, and light, and noise could simply make it break up.

The shards blew back, some flying several feet into the air. And Axelle now ran from side to side, ducking the flying shards, dodging the jagged pieces.

Until she could quite clearly see a pattern.

The rocks, the dirt—all that sealed what was below—started getting piled to the side. Until the center of the floor became clear of rubble.

And that floor . . .

Not rock. Not dirt. More like a viscous membrane. She clung close to the terrible wall with the glistening circuits. But she knew nothing would stay the same here.

No. This was about to change. Things moving, shifting, opening . . .

Yes, something was opening.

And then the membrane began to pull away from itself, actually rip and tear, working its way slowly from the center, then to the outer edges, ever closer to her.

Axelle tried to dig a handhold into the wall, the clanging made by her spare air tank pinging painfully in her ears.

But the smooth wall had also grown slick, covered with a shiny sweaty liquid.

Her nails, her hands were useless as the opening hole of the membrane finally pulled away completely in one final *snap*.

And with that, Axelle's feet gave way, joining the chunks of Martian ground and rock, now sliding down, slowly at first, but then gathering speed, tumbling like a funhouse attraction, sliding down, curving around until her fall finally slowed.

Then she stopped.

She knew that—like it or not—there was no way back up. The only way for her to go was forward, to follow the glowing metallic veins leading ahead, and down.

36

LIEUTENANT HIRAM KOHL LOOKED AT THE MON-
itors that filled the Computer Systems Monitoring
Room. By now, a bunch of scientists should have
joined him here.

Because nothing was working.

He listened as computer voices dully announced
the situation throughout Mars City.

"Central computer system infected. Terminate all
critical procedures immediately."

Right, thought Kohl, as if that were possible. Because . . . that was only *one* of the messages. Then
another, equally dull, dispassionate voice.

"Core failure detected."

Kohl looked at the board. He should send messages to people, but—from here at least—nothing
was getting out.

He spun around and looked at the door. Where the hell were the scientists who were supposed to come here when even the smallest problem happened? And this . . . *this* looked like total failure.

"Collapse of fluid control imminent."

Shit . . .

"Convergence Chamber unstable."

On and on. Kohl licked his lips. *What the hell is going on here?*

And then another thought: *Is there anyone out there? Could he be the last person left alive in Mars City?*

Then the door opened.

Sergeant Kelly took big steps over the dead bodies of what had been some of his best men and women, now piles of bone, skin, and whatever they had in their veins.

One of the newer marines came up to him, eyes all wide, nearly stammering as he spoke.

"Sarge, all secure on the right flank of the lab."

"Right."

The security doors to Delta had been shut down tight. So whatever the hell was going on in there . . . was sealed in there.

And it looked—so far—that most of Delta had been cleared of the marines turned maniacs.

Maniacs . . . is that what they are? he thought.

He heard some chatter from Team Bravo over in Alpha before communications went down in Delta. Calling them zombies.

Idiots. *Zombies.* Like they were in some ancient cheesy horror movie.

Stupid morons.

These guys had been infected. Something from the lab got to them during the explosion. Some disease.

Just a good goddamn thing that he and enough of his marines had dodged it. Somehow immune.

That is, if it was a disease. If it was anything medical.

Funny, though—all the guys who would know something about it were behind the sealed doors of Delta. They'd be the guys to have answers, and the guys to get a cure.

Kelly didn't know the private's name. *They give me too many marines. Too much goddamn responsibility.* "Good. Tell anyone you see to begin a regular patrol. I don't care if we double efforts. Let's make sure there are none of"—he looked down—"these things left stumbling around. Got it?"

The private remained rooted to the spot.

"Okay then—move it!"

Still dazed, the private eventually turned and headed back the way he had come.

Theo forced himself to look up one more time. His mom—the thing that looked like his mom—now only feet away. He screamed at it, hoping that might make it turn away. He could see the skin of the thing through the big gashes of the blouse. The skin all smeared colors, like the paints he used to use in school, smearing them together in a swirl with his fingers.

Closer now. So close.

And he sprang to his feet and started running. Down the corridor. The lights still low.

Running as fast as he could, even though he knew his mother had to be right on his heels.

Kane stopped, sweating now. The cooling systems were down, he guessed. Comm systems down. The whole place falling apart.

And now he saw that the path to the elevator up was blocked by a gas jet shooting fire. No way he could go forward, at least not with the gas torching everything in it path.

He looked up, following the path of the pipe, tracking it to the wall, then down to a control board. Which would, or course, be inoperable. Not until some of the core systems came back online.

But there might be another way.

He followed the pipe some more, looking for a bit of old technology. And then he found it. A small valve with a round handle.

I know how to work that, Kane thought.

He went over there and started to turn the small handle. For a second it didn't budge. More pressure, and it moved only a bit, but enough for Kane to know that he could get it shut. Harder now, hurrying, until he heard the gas jets sputter to nothing and the flames die.

The way to the elevator was clear.

He double-timed it back to the elevator, not even

letting himself wonder what things might be like on top.

But as soon as he got to the doors, he knew that this way up was useless. The blast had kicked in the heavy doors, pushing the twin sheets of metal right into what had been a waiting elevator car.

He took out his PDA. Even with communications down, he assumed he could access material down-loaded. He scrolled to find the Mars City map file.

Searching the underground, and then looking left and right for another way out.

Kane spotted it. Not far. But he also saw that to get to it, a tramway had to be moved into position to cross a gap between two sections of this under-ground area.

He turned on his heels and ran back the way he had come.

Kane watched the mechanical girderlike walkway swing into position. Whatever backup power still worked down here seemed enough to operate the walkway. He let the engine run a few seconds past the connection point to make sure it locked in place.

Then he started across the tram, the freight eleva-tor directly ahead.

When halfway across, something happened. One moment there was nothing ahead of him, and then there was.

He stopped. Something blocked his way.

Not a marine, not a scientist, nothing human.

The head looked to be encased in a metal jacket, but as this thing moved, the metal-like skin of its face moved . . . shifted . . .

But eyes . . . *Does it have eyes?* Those dozens of whitish things—were they eyes? Though it certainly had a mouth. No doubting that. And the legs— massive, ending in giant wedge-shaped claw feet.

It raised its hands. At least it didn't have any weapons. Still, those claws looked nasty.

An alien, Kane thought. *We have aliens here?*

But even as the thing took a towering step close to him, Kane doubted that.

Aliens. Arriving in spaceships? Was that what was happening here?

He raised the shotgun. Whatever the hell it was, Kane was about to blow it off the walkway when he felt something close around his head.

Peripheral vision told him the bad news: another one of those things had appeared the walkway behind him.

And now it held Kane's unhelmeted head firmly in its massive hand, squeezing tight.

Kane quickly brought the muzzle of the gun up and behind him. With the pressure on his skull, he'd be lucky to get off even one shot.

And he hoped that one shot hit something the creature used for an eye.

At first he heard a hard rocklike *thwack,* and Kane knew his shot had only hit its bony head. But the muzzle slipped on that bone skull, and then into something soft.

Kane fired again—and the claw mercifully loosened on Kane's head.

Just as the other creature got to Kane.

He fired the shotgun without aiming, the blast right at the second creature's midsection.

It was flung back—but hard to tell if the blast did any damage. Both creatures were still in the game.

No matter—Kane turned, his finger already clenched tight on the machine gun trigger, as it pumped out an incredible volley of rounds.

Kane made sure the gunfire arced up so the line of bullets curved up to the thing's head. He saw a bunch of shells cut a line across the first creature's skull; the holes immediately began spraying out a thick liquid.

But Kane kept spinning until the same machine gun ride sliced into the second creature, its fingers digging at a crater the shells made in its midsection.

Kane took care that the thing also got a good dose of shells to its head. *Never can have too many head shots . . .*

He watched it tumble forward, then down to its knees.

Then amazingly—the body of the thing began to fade. Until it was gone.

Is this what happened to them when they died, or was it bugging out of here because it was wounded?

He'd leave that for the scientists to figure out. If there were any scientists left.

He finished moving across the walkway to the service elevator, pressed the button, and heard the banging of gears and cables that showed that it was moving.

Then the door opened. And two former space marines stumbled out.

One of them had a right arm in flames, like a torch. Not that it seemed to mind.

"Shit," Kane said.

But Kane hadn't lowered either the machine gun or the high-powered shotgun. He fired both, and the ex-marines fell to either side of Kane.

He quickly got in the elevator, knocked the dead marines' legs out of the way, and hit the button, heading back to the main floor.

Kane hesitated as the elevator doors opened. Best not to simply walk out without taking a look around. The door began to close again, and Kane hit a button, forcing it back open.

All clear and quiet here.

Kane stepped out. He lay the shotgun against the wall and dug out his PDA. He scrolled down to a name.

Suddenly the earpiece came to life. Communications must be back.

"Kane? Where the hell are you?" Kelly, sounding a bit stressed.

"On the main level, Sergeant. Heading to—"

The sound of scattered bullets.

"Scratch that, Kane. I want you to get to Administration, check damages, set up patrols. Anyone who's still okay, get them patrolling the full perimeter around Admin."

Kane felt he should ask, *Why me? Aren't there some senior people around, some smart-ass lieutenants, some crack PFCs?* Instead: "You want *me* to do this?"

Kelly hesitated. "Shit, yeah. I know where you came from. Put your goddamn skills to use, Kane."

"Got it. And how are you there?"

"Just doing cleanup. Delta is sealed, so that's okay. Got my team here checking every damn corridor."

Kane thought of Maria. "And Team Bravo?"

"Doing the same in Alpha. Looks like that's all okay too. Get hustling, Kane."

"Right."

The radio went quiet. But before he started, he hit an icon on the PDA, and the earpiece came to life again.

"Yeah?"

"Maria? It's Kane."

"Kane, you okay? You catch any shit down below?"

"You might say that. But I'm up here, going to Admin. You okay?"

"Yeah. Could use an officer or three, but we got everyone spread out. Looks like the thing is over."

Kane thought of the creature on the walkway—appearing, then vanishing. *Over?* He wasn't too sure of that.

He whispered through his gasping, heavy breaths. "Yes?"

"Campbell here. They're getting systems back online, counselor. But any deep space comm is still going to depend on your getting there, creating a secure channel, and getting the word out to the armada. Where are you now?"

Though it was just a voice in his head, Swann shook his head. His voice was annoyed, raspy.

"I—I don't know. I haven't checked the layout in a bit. B-but I'm going the right way."

Nothing for a second. Then: "Good. Just stay calm. You got to be pretty close. Just let me know when you're there, okay?"

Another pointless nod. Then: "Yes. I will." And Swann took some more cautious steps down the corridor.

Kohl looked at the two scientists who had entered the room. Ignoring him, they went to the monitors and began talking to each other.

"We can divert to a different energy processor. And reroute the dedicated power from the Hydrocon—at least temporarily."

"Deep Space Comm will need a separate feed."

"Yeah, we can do that."

Then one of them looked at Kohl. "Lieutenant, we're going to need another pair of hands in here as we change things. Just do what we say, okay?"

"Sure," Kohl said, but the scientist turned away without waiting for an answer.

. . .

"Right. Good. Just keep me fully informed."

General Hayden looked away from the screen floating above his conference table and then right at Campbell.

"A fucking mess, Campbell. And we don't know what the hell happened? This may take down the entire Mars project."

Hayden waited for Campbell to answer, but the UAC security chief just looked around the room, as if sizing it up.

"General, we don't want to make any advance judgments on what may or may not happen, okay? We would of course like to know what the hell *did* happen today. If it's a virus, there will be issues of quarantine, protection . . . I assume we can eventually get access to all of Delta's video and—"

A blast of gunfire from outside, and Campbell stopped.

"Christ," Hayden said, "I thought we had this area secure."

"Guess not that secure."

Hayden turned back to the holo screen. His finger jabbed at it as if stabbing someone. "I said I wanted updates on any activity in this sector. When you say secure, goddamn it, you better mean secure."

Then back to Campbell.

"Cleaning up?" Campbell said.

"Right."

"And General, I'm going to set up shop here, during the crisis. If you don't mind."

The bastard, Hayden thought. *Taking over just because he has Kelliher's backing.* "You're going to stay here?"

"Yeah. Once Comm is fully up and operational, I'll want full access." A beat. "Your access."

"I will have a lot to—"

"Don't worry. I won't get in your way. And General, I even showed up with a little something to make us both feel better."

Campbell pointed to a large metal crate that had just been delivered minutes before.

"A little insurance policy—just in case . . ."

Hayden was about to ask what was in the crate, but then decided that—for now—he didn't even want to know.

Kane kept running in the direction of the scream, now horribly aware that it was the shrill and terrified sound made by a kid.

He turned a corner and didn't see anything. But he kept up his pace and came to another turn, to a corridor that didn't look like it led anywhere.

Another scream echoed horribly. Kane took the corner and kept running, sweat dripping off him, the air growing thick and heavy with the environmental systems down.

Then, at the end, he turned and saw the boy. Curled up tight into a corner, yelling.

"Son, it's okay. You're going to—"

The boy interrupted his screaming for just a moment to point . . . right past Kane, behind him, to the other hall that led into this cul-de-sac.

Kane turned. It was one of those things. Someone who used to be okay, Now, a stumbling creature ready to attack. He could see what was left of a woman's clothing—patches of mottled skin exposed. The hair shooting out wildly from the skull. One eye drooped as if it had been damaged, the poached-egg eyeball rolling around in its socket. A long thick dark tongue lolled out of its mouth. The teeth—exposed to their roots—now all cracked, with sharp edges.

Mom . . .

Kane lowered his guns to her, then thought of the boy. He couldn't. No fucking way. Not in front of the kid.

He turned to the boy, quickly. His voice no longer soothing or reassuring.

"Start running, son. Down there—the direction I came from."

The boy didn't move. Only seconds left.

"Start moving now!" Kane yelled, hoping that his voice alone could make the kid get up and move.

The mother-thing kept coming, its one good eye straying from her son to Kane.

Then, amazingly, Kane heard movement from behind.

He lowered his voice: "That's it. Just start running. And run as fast as you can."

Kane felt the boy whiz behind him, then the out-of-place sound of steps running down the hall.

He snapped back to the problem at hand. He took the butt of the shotgun and carefully charged the zombie, smacking the gun butt into its jaw.

It made only the slightest of grunting noises.

But then it recoiled, which Kane knew too well meant that the thing was going to jump at him. The boy's steps receded, faded, until Kane couldn't hear them anymore.

The kid was gone. And the mother was about to fly.

"Sorry . . ." Kane whispered, not knowing to whom . . . or why.

He pumped two rounds into the thing's head. Large chunks of skull went flying away. Then, since it still wobbled around like—God—it could still move—he fired a third round. And finally, in its tattered and stained rags, what was left of the boy's mother fell to her knees, then forward.

His earpiece crackled on. "Kane? You there yet?"

"Almost, Sergeant . . . almost."

38

AS KANE ENTERED THE ADMINISTRATION AREA, he could see that chaos still ruled here. The floor was still dotted with bodies of things that had either been destroyed in the blast or transformed into the creatures, then shot.

Civilians huddled together, wide-eyed, looking as if someone might slaughter them next. The few space marines in the area kept whipping their heads right and left, the fear blatantly obvious.

They're immobilized, Kane thought. Frozen troops huddled like they were stranded on an iceberg.

Kane touched his earpiece, and immediately heard Kelly's voice. "Yes?"

"I'm here. It's a mess."

"Right. Un-mess it. Get that area secure, Kane."

"Yup." He disconnected from Kelly, then walked

over to one group of marines. "Okay, listen up. I don't care whether you're new here, or you've been on Mars for a year, we are going to get this area patrolled."

They looked at Kane.

"W-wait a minute," a young guy with wide eyes spoke up. "Who says? We should stay right here. Till some brass tells us."

Kane took a step toward the jarhead. "I'm telling you what's going to happen." Then a look at the others standing around. "We're going to do this, and we're going to do this now, understand? In two-person patrols. Report in every five minutes. Watch each other's back. And Christ"—he looked at one marine who had only a handgun—"make sure you got some serious firepower. Shotguns, machine guns. You'll need more than toys to deal with those things."

Kane waited. They'd either respond to his assuming command, or continue fighting it, whining. Then things might get a little nasty.

But then, one by one, the heads nodded.

"Okay, good. Pair up. Start now. Decide which sector each team will do."

Kane then moved over to another cluster of marines and delivered the same news. Luckily, they had seen the others follow Kane's lead, so they fell into line immediately.

They're all scared, Kane knew. But they each knew that the best way to stay alive was to work together. Just like what was happening now.

He stopped two marines. "You two. I want you to stay on guard here. Just make sure the civilians stay calm. Don't let anyone back to their offices or rooms until we get an all clear."

More nods. Kane was thinking, *Maybe this mess is all over,* when a woman came up to him, sobbing, heaving, grabbing Kane's arm.

He turned to her. One of the receptionists, looking about as rocked as one can be.

"Yes?"

"My friend, Jane—she works with me. She felt sick, she went to the restroom."

Kane took a breath. "Alone?"

The woman nodded. "I—I didn't want to go. I was—"

"And where is that?"

She pointed down to a corridor past reception, heading toward Central Access.

Another breath. "I'll go check."

The woman nodded. A bit of a smile. Though Kane doubted he'd be bringing back any good news.

Kane pushed opened the door to the restroom. An overhead light sputtered, now flickering bright, then fading to darkness.

For a moment, he remained at the threshold. He hadn't survived this day so far by rushing into things before he knew what the hell was happening.

He heard a heaving, wet sound. Deep breaths. Coming from down the end, near the last stall.

The lights sputtered out.

Damn, I better get a headlight. Something I can wear in case this whole place goes dark.

The lights flickered on again, the wet, huffing sound constant. Maybe the receptionist was okay.

"Jane?" he said.

The wet sound stopped. But there was no answer.

Funny about taboos, he thought. This room, forbidden to men. Even now, even today.

Again: "Jane?"

This time the sound continued, and Kane started a slow walk deeper into the room, past stalls where the doors were half open.

When he got near the end, he saw blood stains on the floor. From the woman, from some other unlucky person, or—

The lights flickered out.

He heard movement. And this time, the lights stayed out.

Instinctively, Kane took a small step backward. *Something moving.*

When the lights came on again, he could see what it was. And it was something *new. . . .*

The lights strobed, but he saw the four-legged thing in front of him. It had the woman's neck, now stringy, tight in its bulldoglike jaws, still chewing as its head bobbed up and down, unperturbed by Kane's presence.

It threw back its jaws, and what was left of the

woman's head went flying into its mammoth maw.

The front of the thing had a carapace with a slight reddish-pink color, unless that was from all the blood.

But the rear—narrow legs made of steel.

Metal legs . . .

Kane took another step back. *The thing is part machine. Part goddamn robot, or—*

Kane fired a quick look to his rear. Wouldn't be too great to be sandwiched between two of these things.

But nothing was behind him. At least not yet.

Kane looked down to the thing's forepaws, looking like forked hooves ending in sharp, stiletto-like points.

Nice weapon, and the teeth? No animal on Earth had teeth like that . . .

Another step back.

Weirdly he thought, *Nice doggie . . .*

The thing seemed stupid, finishing its meal before concentrating on Kane.

But with a teeth-cleaning swipe of its tongue, it leapt toward Kane. And though he jumped to the right, ramming into a row of sinks, he felt one of those front claws slice into his left thigh.

The pain sent a spike into his brain. A few more jabs like that and he could join the dead girl on the floor.

He pointed his machine gun at the thing, hesitating just a fraction of a second: where to aim?

The head resembled the hard shell of a long-prehistoric deepsea arachnid. The mouth too, and the eyes, maybe the machine legs in the back.

Or, hell, maybe *all of it.*

An ancient monster.

He started spraying bullets at the thing, the room filling with smoke from the ejected shells. The pink thing opened its mouth—you could fit a bowling ball into the space easily.

Kane just kept firing as if spray-painting the creature with bullets.

And then he noticed—it wasn't trying to advance.

It wasn't quite dead. Reflexes or something kept the tongue moving, an eye twitching. The right leg trembled a bit as if also trying to move.

But Kane realized—it was about as dead as the thing was going to get. And it was beyond hurting anyone else.

He turned and walked out. Best tell everyone to find another restroom to use. At least until that one was cleaned up.

Back at Administration he could see that the civilian workers still clustered together. But now there were marine guards looking alert. In his ear he heard the teams checking in as they reached each juncture of this part of Mars City.

And the reassuring words . . .

All secure here . . .

Kane hit his communicator.

"Looking okay here, Sergeant."

Kelly laughed. "Here too, Kane. Good work. Now maybe someone will tell us what the hell happened."

Maybe . . .

"Right, Sergeant. I'm going to check the patrols."

"Okay, Kane. And when this is over, you and me . . . we gotta have a talk."

When it's over?

And Kane thought—hoped—that *that* time was right now.

He thought about praying.

But he'd given that up a long time ago.

39

HAYDEN LOOKED AT CAMPBELL.

"All secure. Should make your boss happy."

"That's your boss too. *When* he hears it. Does this"—he pointed at the smart board on the right wall—"thing work at all?"

"Sure."

Campbell went to the board and touched it, and the board gave off a soft glow. A small menu appeared on the side of the electronic board, but Campbell ignored that.

"So General, let's see what we've been dealing with here. There are these—" Campbell used his finger to quickly sketch what looked like a human soldier. "What used to be your space marines."

"Zombies. They've started calling them 'zombies.'"

"Funny. So right, and then there's the citizen version of the same thing." Campbell fired Hayden a glance. "Which has the advantage—for us at least—that they don't carry any weapons."

Then Campbell drew something long and spindly, giving it pointy ears.

"What the hell is that?" Hayden asked.

"What a few of your people described."

"Looks like a giant bug or—"

"Yeah. Whatever. General, either way, it's something that wasn't here before. It's not one of your Mars citizens transformed."

"I guess so, but—"

Campbell turned back to the board and drew something resembling a dog, only with oversized forepaws and a head that seemed fused to its body.

"And this—supposedly a bloody pink in front. Machine legs in the back."

"Only been two of them seen. They called them 'pinkies.'"

"Right. Now"—he faced Hayden directly—"now my question. Looking at these, how do we know there aren't *more* things, other things out there?"

Hayden shook his head. "Because we haven't seen them. We haven't seen anything else . . ."

Then Campbell, his eyes still fixed on Hayden, added the unsaid word.

" . . . yet."

Swann reached the giant Comm Center and saw that already people had begun moving about normally—as if it was another day at work.

"Excuse me," he said, grabbing one woman in a white coat moving quickly through the lab, "is this place . . . operational yet?"

The woman shook her head. Swann noticed her name. E. Tharp.

"Not yet. We're still running tests, rerouting power from the secondary energy units. But I guess we should be ready to try a deep space transmission soon."

"We have to do it now."

The woman smiled. "Oh really? And you are?"

"Elliot Swann, counsel for the UAC and personal representative of Ian Kelliher. A message *must* go out right away."

As soon as he said the words, Swann realized how pompous they sounded.

But Kelliher's name seemed to have an effect.

"Well, let me see what I can do. You can take a seat over there, at the main consoles. When the system's ready, you can broadcast away."

Swann walked over and sat down, feeling safe for the first time since the incident.

He shook his head.

The incident . . .

Maria leaned against the wall. Andy Kim came over.

"You did good. Got this place all buttoned down. Bet there's a promotion in this for you."

"Good. That's just what I want. A promotion and another tour of duty up here." She realized how whiny her words must have sounded. "Everyone getting the bodies removed?"

"Yeah—we gave the job to the newbies. Some of them gagging, throwing up." Kim nodded. "Pretty damn messy."

Maria nodded. When would Kelly get someone over here to really take charge?

She thought of Kane. Maybe back in Admin, maybe still fighting his way up from the Mars undercity. A dangerous place and a dangerous time to give a damn about someone.

Kim saw the look on her face.

"You okay?"

Another nod. "I'm just fine," she lied.

"What was the last message from Betruger?" Campbell asked.

"Said Delta was all okay. The doors locked for security. Nothing more since. Think whatever failures are going on in there are interfering with local communication. We have people on it, though."

Suddenly Swann's voice filled the room.

"We're . . . all set here. We finally have deep space comm ready."

Hayden looked at Campbell. "So now, what? We get the fleet to come? Reinforce us? Save our goddamn—"

Campbell held up a hand.

"Good work, counselor. But there's been a change. Everything seems under control here. So a new mes-

sage to go out. And then tell them to get busy rerouting the comm system do we can talk from here."

The hesitation in Swann's voice was clear.

"A different message?"

Campbell looked at Hayden, and the general
shrugged.

"Ask the armada to assume a near-Mars orbit position but emphasize to them that there is no current
need for their help or support, that"—another look
at Hayden—"that . . . everything is under control
here."

"And Mr. Kelliher?"

"I'll prepare a full report, to be sent once we have
the full comm system back up. Understand?"

"Yes. Though—"

"Great. Now send it."

The radio went quiet.

"Tell me, General—you got any bourbon? Been a
mighty long day so far."

Hayden leaned down to a locked cabinet behind
his desk and pulled out a bottle.

Campbell laughed. "Ah, I knew Mars was in good
hands . . ."

Kane looked around. The receptionist still shook and
sobbed, sitting at her desk.

But other than that—and the sound of bodies
being put into bags designed for waste and zipped
up—the chaos, the smell of fear in the air, had
faded.

Of course, if he were in charge there'd be more than a couple of things that would worry him.

Team Bravo was all the way over in Alpha. If anything happened there, getting to them would take a while.

Never did like having my troops scattered.

Whoa, he thought. *My* troops? No way any of these grunts up here were his troops.

Then there was Kelly all the way over by Delta.

All secure, he said, but the lab . . . still sealed up tight.

Until they got in there and assessed what the hell had happened, what the status was—then Kelly and his marines were effectively pinned. Leaving Kane and the scattered force here.

Technically Hayden was in charge, and he probably would try to find a lieutenant alive somewhere to run operations.

But for now, as if by instinct, they looked at Kane.

At least, Kane thought, it was quiet now.

Quiet . . .

He saw a scattering of brightly colored chairs over by reception.

He grabbed his shotgun, which had been lying against the wall, and walked over. Now he could feel the intense muscle pain from the insanity of his fights below. Jabs and sparks of pain shooting into him with every step.

The bandage he had put on his leg gash already showed pink through the gauze and tape.

He walked to a chair. Bright orange, and shaped like a melted teacup.

And Private John Kane sat down.

The siege—or whatever it was—was over.

He sat down because there was this secret rule in combat. When the fighting ended—even for a few minutes—always sit down when you can.

'Cause you never know . . .

THE
ILLUSION

40

THE LIGHTS SPUTTERED AGAIN AND THEN STAYED full on.

MacDonald looked up, the room, the mayhem, the bodies, the creatures—

(The creatures . . .)

—now fully lit.

But with that burst of full power, he watched Pod One, which had grown quiet, now suddenly emitting a screeching sound, like massive metallic gears scraping, grinding.

A brilliant red glow began in the pod.

(Which MacDonald knew wasn't a pod anymore, not a scientific device anymore. It was something *else*.)

And as that glow bloomed, MacDonald could see,

from his fetal position curled up behind an over-turned table, a figure begin to appear, then emerge.

He saw Betruger, his skin reflecting the reddish color, or perhaps that glow came from him.

Only now Dr. Malcolm Betruger no longer held something in his hands.

MacDonald risked lifting his head to get a better look.

The object was gone—and now MacDonald *remembered* that object. U1—from Site 3. An unknown object with an unknown purpose. Or what used to be unknown.

Gone somewhere, and now Betruger walked amid the beings in the room, grunting, shuffling, moving aside . . . making a path for him.

He walked to the sealed doors of Delta Lab.

MacDonald knew what Betruger was about to do. In minutes those doors would open. And what was inside Delta would come out . . .

PALO ALTO, CALIFORNIA

Ian Kelliher sat at his desk. The reassuring message from the commander of the joint UAC/USA armada did nothing to calm him.

No, not until he knew in detail what had happened on Mars—what may still be happening—he would not be reassured in the slightest. But with deep space communication still—apparently—limited, there wasn't much he could do.

A holo-screen floated above his desk. Kelliher touched the air and saw the face of a man, an employee of Kelliher's based here that the precious Dr. Betruger didn't know about.

And not only didn't know about, but would be livid if he found about it.

"Yes, Dr. Simonsen?"

"Sir, in light of the issues on Mars, do you want us to put a hold on further experiments?"

The experiments, secret, replicating what Kelliher's team imagined Betruger to be doing on Mars.

"No. I think we can be properly . . . cautious. But stopping? I don't think so, Dr. Simonsen."

"Yes, sir. Thank you."

The screen vanished from the air.

At least, he thought, *everything is now secure on Mars. There will be investigations, reports, maybe even disciplinary action against Betruger or his team. All quite manageable stuff.*

He nodded.

Totally manageable . . .

INFIRMARY STORAGE ROOM, MARS CITY

Theo looked around the room filled with boxes and crates. With symbols and words he didn't understand.

He had a thought. There's nowhere safe here. Not in this room, not out there.

Look what happened to his mother. How she got sick. Something bad happening to her.

And the same thing could happen to me!

He heard voices outside the door. They all sounded okay. But what if they weren't?

The voices came closer.

Theo looked around the room, then up. He saw an opening in the ceiling. Small, but he could fit—he was sure of it. No one would look for him up there. No one could fit in that small space. But where did it lead?

The voices became even louder.

Carefully, Theo began climbing up the shelves, taking care to be as quiet as he could. He had climbed trees back home, always careful not to put his weight on a branch that could snap, sending him flying down.

He got to the top. Then, with a last look at the dark room, he crawled into the opening, pulling himself up, and in . . .

Until he was gone.

SITE 3—BEYOND THE CAVE

Nowhere to go, Axelle thought, *but straight ahead.* She had forced herself to ignore the grid of pulsing lines all around the walls of this . . . place.

Dreamlike. Surreal. And all that pulsing—as if sensing that she was coming.

Like—like—

She thought of an old movie: a young girl walking on a curling yellow pathway into the unknown.

Nothing else alive here. Unless—

(Just a thought, really . . .)

This whole place was alive.

She looked at the air level of her suit. Low. She'd need the spare tank soon. Her last tank. Either way, she wouldn't be able to survive here for long.

Time was about to run out.

Her attempts to communicate with Mars City had proved useless, as if Mars City didn't exist anymore, wasn't anywhere on the surface here—as if she was thousands and thousands of light-years away from the dead Red Planet.

Then, ending the sense of being alone, more sounds.

Penetrating her helmet. Sounds. Voices almost. Except no one ever heard voices like that.

She stopped. The thought: *How silly. There's nowhere else to go, nowhere to walk but straight ahead.*

ADMINISTRATION—MARS CITY

John Kane watched everyone moving, their speed increasing as the fear receded.

Fear . . .

Was there anything worse?

And as he remained seated, ignoring the pain that wracked his body, sitting just a few more precious minutes before he'd have to once again stand—

He wondered if everyone realized what the worst fear was. The fear of what was yet to come.

For now, Kane kept that thought to himself.

ABOUT THE AUTHOR

Matthew Costello's work includes innovative and critically acclaimed novels, games, and television. His novel *Beneath Still Waters* was filmed by Lionsgate last year, and his latest novel, *Nowhere,* was published in 2007. He's written for PBS, The Disney Channel, The Sci-Fi Channel, and the BBC among others. He's scripted dozens of bestselling and award-winning games including *The 7th Guest, Doom 3,* and *Pirates of the Caribbean: At World's End.* You can learn more at www.mattcostello.com.

Printed in the United States
By Bookmasters